ASHTABULA TO YANBU

Rosemary Day

Published by FastPencil

Published by FastPencil
307 Orchard City Drive
Suite 210
Campbell CA 95008 USA
info@fastpencil.com
(408) 540-7571
(408) 540-7572 (Fax)
http://www.fastpencil.com

This is a work of fiction.

Rosemary Day would appreciate your comments on her novel. rosemaryday777@gmail.com

Printed in the United States of America.

First Edition

TO DDRN

❧

Chapter 1

Sunday, September 13, 1987

At the Yanbu Airport I am taken to the VIP lounge and told to wait here until my sponsor comes to claim me. Un-VIP like, the furnishings are as unremarkable as a small-town American dentist's bland waiting room—minus the picture of lips and teeth hanging on a wall with some silly motivating caption like: When you finish eating your food, your food starts to eat your teeth. Another difference, there are no magazines on the chrome and glass coffee table. I am the only VIP in this quiet lounge, and I don't expect anyone will dash in and ask if I'd like a cocktail. I keep going over and over the incident in the Jeddah Airport. I lost control and struck his face with unbelievable force. He provoked me. The way he looked at me. I decide to fret about something else.

I will be late for my new job. Given the strict enforcement of rules that I read about in the Survival Guide to Saudi Arabia and what I have already experienced, I can't help but worry. How late am I? I am in no shape to calculate time changes. I'll explain that I missed my plane. It was the fault of the airport guys. I can't believe I'm on the defensive and I haven't set one foot in the hospital.

After an hour has passed, a tall, thin man in a white and flowing headdress anchored with a black cord and wearing a long white robe introduces himself to me. I don't catch his name—it's something I've never heard before. He tells me he is my ride to the hospital. He doesn't offer to carry my big, overstuffed suitcase, so I ask him to give me a hand with it. We lift it into the trunk of a white compact that looks like it crossed the desert more than a few times. As I open the door to the back seat, he says, "Sit up front." I close the back door. I organize myself, (a long skirt and large black tote) in the front seat and I am faced with a sign on the dashboard: Males Only—Females Back Seat.

"What about this?" I point to the sign.

"No problem. I know the police," says the man whose name I didn't catch.

As we ride along in an uneasy silence, I stare straight ahead. I see two things only: sky and sand. One infinite wall of blue. One shade of blue—sky blue. No clouds, no trees, no buildings. One endless carpet of sand. One shade of sand—pale yellow. No posted road signs, no cars passing, no gas stations. The emptiness of the desert deepens the emptiness within me. I am acutely aware that I'm far from home, and that, I'm in a small compact driven by a tall stranger in a vast desert.

I decide to take a good look at this stranger. His olive complexion is marred by deep pockmarks, his lashes are thick, long, and black, his nose—perfectly straight. He doesn't wear sunglasses in spite of the intense sunlight. "Are you scared?" he asks.

"No sir, I'm not."

"My name is Moktar."

"Muckter." I repeat.

"Moktar." He returns the volley.

"Okay, Moktar. I just didn't like the way you asked that question—I'm sorry I mispronounced your name."

I suppose he could rip my clothes off and rape me, throw my body on hot sand, run this little white compact back and forth over me until my face is unrecognizable, all organs crushed, every bone broken, all life gone. Then vultures will picnic and fight among themselves until I am really all gone. My poor elderly parents would have to live out their final days never knowing what happened to their cherished and only child. No Irish wake, no Catholic funeral mass, no tender and loving eulogies—nothing—absolutely nothing. My parents' life savings wiped out as they are duped by hucksters who promise they will find Kelly and bring her home safely.

Moktar will sell my United States of America passport, my first and only one. On the flight from New York to Madrid, I studied my prized possession. On the first page, there is one forty-six word sentence.

"The Secretary of State of the United States hereby requests all whom it may concern to permit the citizen/national of the United States named herein to pass without delay or hindrance and in case of need to give all lawful aid and protection."

Moktar informs me he has to stop at a police station. We pull off the highway onto a dirt road, ride for five more minutes, then stop in front of a one-story grey and crumbling concrete building. He leaves the air conditioner on as he goes to take care of business.

Moktar returns. We drive another fifteen minutes or so when we come into an area that looks like the planned community I saw on the brochure that the recruiter sent me. Palm trees line the un-potholed streets. Smooth sidewalks, and green shrubs outline fresh, white low-rise buildings. I feel some relief. I powder my nose, freshen my lipstick, and brush my long tangled hair. We reach the hospital at last, and I'm pleased that it is a small modern one-story white structure. I'm elated at the sight of something familiar.

I go to get out of the compact and Moktar orders me to "wait here." After what seems like an eternity, he returns and introduces me to the chief of housekeeping services, a Filipino woman in her early forties whose name is Fidelis Velasquez. Moktar drives us to Camp Five (the female workers' enclave), which is a maze of connected one-story housing units that look like cream-colored matchboxes. The ride is brief and without conversation. Fidelis and I climb out of the car, gather my stuff, and lug it to my designated unit number 5350.

Fidelis unlatches a courtyard gate and to my horror a bunch of scrawny cats lie around the front door of the residence. "Shit! Good God, those damn things took me by surprise." I grab Fidelis's arm. "Please get them out of here. Hurry, hurry, open the door. Jesus Christ, open the door!" I slam the door behind us.

"Oh my God, Fidelis, I apologize for the outburst."

She looks at me with grave concern and asks, "What happened?"

"I have a severe, I mean severe, really severe, allergy to cats. I mean life-threatening. How many were there?"

"Just a few, maybe three or four. Now, let's get you settled."

I sink into an ugly brown chair. I look around the room.

"Again, I apologize for the outburst. I didn't mean to scare you."

"Are you all right now?"

"No, I mean yes. Fidelis, this place is dirty. The walls look like they haven't been painted in years. The arm on this chair is broken. The lamps look like balloons hanging from the ceiling of a gymnasium on prom night. Look at the carpet. I'm so disappointed in these accommodations."

Fidelis moves over to the hideous maroon drapes and parts them. The blast of sunlight serves only to highlight the dust and grime on furniture that belongs in a dumpster. She says, "You'll feel better after you get some rest—take a short nap. I'll be back in an hour to take you to the commissary. After that we'll return to the hospital and take it from there."

I walk around this dreary excuse of an apartment feeling increasingly miserable. Pink Formica countertops with brown scum in the cracks flank a steel sink. The drain basket is the resting place of three wrinkled lima beans. I go into the bedroom. I really don't feel comfortable undressing here. I leave the bedroom fully clothed, and fall asleep on the foul-smelling black couch, dotted with cigarette burns.

. . .

Fidelis rings my doorbell in less than an hour.

"Come in, Fidelis. I'm a little out of it from all the travel. What is the date and time?"

"It's Sunday, September 13, 1:35 p.m. to be exact. I have some riyals for you. You can repay me when it's convenient."

"Thank you." I feel like bursting into tears. She is kind and her kindness feels good. She has a pretty round face and soft brown eyes.

"Please sit down. I want to tell you something." Fidelis sits on the chair with the broken arm. I sit on the stinking ugly couch. "About the cat thing, I really don't have an allergy to them. I have cat phobia. It's a neurotic thing. I'm not crazy. I just have an irrational fear of cats. That's the only one I have, really. Some people are afraid of spiders, dogs, birds, fish, ponies, enclosed spaces, open spaces, all kinds of things."I understand." She pauses, and then says, "I am sorry to tell you the camps are overrun with cats."

"Fidelis, I specifically asked about cats when I did telephone interviews with several Americans who once worked in Saudi Arabia. Everyone, I mean every interviewee denied or didn't recall seeing cats in residential areas. Some recalled stray cats in small old towns, but just a few."

"I think this area, Camp Five in particular, has a big problem with stray cats. Many of the nurses like to feed the cats. We can go to the commissary now."

"Fidelis, I'll be just a little jumpy because I'll have to be looking out for cats. Will you shoo them away for me?"

"Of course."

It's quiet and the air is hot. I see cats at a distance. They are small and thin—black, brown, beige. I can't believe my misfortune.

Fidelis is attempting to tell me how to take a shortcut to the commissary but I can't concentrate on that. I must watch out for the cats. "Look over there, Fidelis. I'm okay as long as the cats don't get any closer."

The streets and sidewalks are neat and orderly. There are no billboards, no posted signs, no bus stops, and no traffic lights. The only vehicles are the security patrol jeeps.

The housing units are all the same. There is a gated courtyard at the front entrance and at the side is a small yard that can be accessed thru sliding glass doors in the living room. The units are fenced in by rows of closely planted shrubs and are numbered but there are no mailboxes. Fidelis explains that we pick up our mail at the hospital.

The air-conditioned commissary is a welcome relief from the oppressive heat and blasting sun and cats. Shelves crowded with imported canned goods line three narrow aisles that terminate at the checkout counter and cash register. I buy a jar of peanut butter, a can of tuna, a box of tea bags, six bottles of water, a box of saltine crackers, and a box of soap powder. It seems the commissary is organized to meet the needs of Westerners. It reminds me of a neighborhood store offering just what you need to get by. In other words, it's not a super-market. I slip the change into my skirt pocket without any idea of the cost of my first meal in Yanbu.

The walk back to 5350 is as terrifying as the walk to the commis-sary. There are a hell of a lot of cats here.

Fidelis waits while I put the groceries away and then we step out of unit 5350. Hot air slaps my face. Once we exit the Camp Five maze, it looks like a straight shot along one street to the hospital. I estimate we've got a half-mile in front of us. It's very quiet—just a few cars pass by and we are the only pedestrians.

"Kelly, when we get to the hospital, I'll introduce you to Angelita. She runs the administrative offices. She'll show you to your office."

I mumble, "Sounds good."

The cold chill of the air-conditioned hospital along with its medic-inal odor is welcoming. I'm introduced to Angelita who looks like a Vidal Sassoon model. She's a Filipino who must be a size three. Her hair, which looks like it's been dipped in black ink, sprouts from her tiny head and ends at her shoulders in a fashionable blunt cut. She takes me to my office.

It is simple and clean: an office desk, desk lamp, swivel chair, and a four-drawer stacked steel gray file cabinet. In front of a picture window there is a round table with three matching straight-back chairs. The plum is the view out of the window. A magenta bougain-villea vine graces a wall of a small courtyard. A backless bench for two is on the right and a wooden latched door is on the left. It's picture perfect.

"It's a lovely oasis."

Angelita smiles, places her hand on my shoulder and says, "Your first appointment is with Mr. Al Kahairi for his infamous orientation session."

"Infamous?"

Angelita winks, removes her hand from my shoulder, and continues, "Mr. Al Kahairi is a little strange. My Advice—don't ask questions, just listen." She points with her delicate forefinger and says in a whisper, "three doors down on the left."

I can't wait to hear this. I take a deep breath in—let it slowly out and walk three doors down.

"Hello, Mr. Al Kahairi. I'm here for the orientation session."

A sizeable figure wearing the traditional white headdress anchored with a black cord and a long white robe rises from a chair, comes out from behind a large mahogany desk and walks across the room. Due in part to intense sunlight streaming in from a picture window and also to his too tight white robe that hugs his bulky midsection, I am afforded a clear view of a large apron of adipose tissue, an impression of a big belly button, and an outline of boxer shorts. I feel like laughing and crying.

After a stroll around the office, he seats himself in an upholstered armchair. He takes a deep breath, lets it out slowly, joins his chubby hands together and rests them on his mountainous belly. His fat toes bulge out of his leather sandals. He tilts his head, his fleshy jowls sway. "Welcome to the Kingdom of Saudi Arabia."

"Thank you, I am happy to be here."

"Did you bring the twenty passport pictures with you?"

"No, was I supposed to?"

"Yes, yes, of course." He's upset with me. "This is very important. Security requirements. You should have been instructed to bring twenty passport pictures with you."

"I am sorry, sir, but …"

He gets up. He grabs the phone on his desk, punches in numbers, and begins shouting in Arabic. Finally, his rant comes to an abrupt end. He lowers the receiver into the cradle and sits in the chair behind the big desk. I feel like sobbing, but I will myself not to.

"Miss Day, the first order of business is to get you an Igama."

"A what, sir? I beg your pardon?"

"The Igama is like your passport, except it is written in Arabic. This is necessary because most of the security men cannot read English. They, the Security, may stop you at any time and ask for identification. The Igama services this purpose. To be without your Igama creates suspicion. The Security may think you sold it to a terrorist. You would be investigated: that takes a long time, and it would be very inconvenient for you. Moktar will have to take you downtown to get your picture taken."

He shuffles papers and mutters, "the authorities do not like delays like this. You must carry the Igama with you at all times. If you are stopped and don't have it, you will go to jail. I repeat. You will be investigated and that takes a long time. It would be very inconvenient for you."

"Okay, I get it about the Igama, but I don't understand why I can't have my passport. Why, may I ask, is the hospital holding my passport?"

His glare says it all. He's angry about the twenty pictures and now I'm asking a direct question. I think I just struck out with my new boss.

"Miss Day, in Saudi Arabia there are many foreigners. Passports from certain countries are considered extremely valuable. So theft is a problem. The employers keep the passports of their workers as a protection." He looks like a pious monk desiring only to protect the unprotected. He reaches into a desk drawer and grabs a handful of individually wrapped candies, tosses them on the desk, and says, "help yourself." He unwraps a piece, stares at it, pushes it to the side. He looks sad. I feel sad.

He straightens his shoulders and begins again. "Now about the rules for the girls."

"Mister Al Kahairi, who are you talking about?"

"Your nurses. The girls who live in Camp Five. There are rules—lots of rules. The girls are forbidden to go to the male camps. They should never wander into the male camps, even if they are riding their bikes to get exercise. This is suspicious. Suspicion leads to investigation. Investigations are time-consuming, laborious. Inconvenient.

"They should never go to the married camps. House sitting for married couples while they're on leave is strictly forbidden. Not long ago one of the girls was house sitting and Security needed to enter because a water pipe broke. They found liquor and fancy sleeping dresses in the house. This is bad—very suspicious. The girl was investigated. The girls are only authorized to work in the hospital. Only men are authorized to house sit.

"The girls are not authorized to sleep anywhere but in their own unit. This is the rule. If the Authority finds out about these things, we look bad. The girls should not go from one apartment to another within the camp in their pajamas. They should be dressed decently."

I bite a fingernail. I wish I didn't do that. But these rules are making me nervous. I should be asking about the budgeted positions for the nursing department.

"Questions, Miss Day?"

"Well, I, I never imagined that "separation of the sexes" could possibly have such far reaching effects. I guess I had no idea how that would play out in everyday life. I mean, I read that in the world of Islam there is no distinction between a secular life and a religious one. But I ...""

"Let's move on, Miss Day." He smiles. "The girls in Camp Five must obey the curfew. They may not be out on the streets between ten o'clock at night and six in the morning. If they need to go to the hospital for example, as do night shift workers, they must take the hospital shuttle bus—no exceptions."

Then, with a relaxed half-smile, he says, "If the girls get hungry after ten in the evening, (after curfew) they can order something from the Pizza Palace. It is the only restaurant authorized to deliver to Camp Five. We are flexible."

"Indeed," I mumble.

"So, Miss Day, you must have some questions."

"You've covered so much."

"There is a lot to cover." He is so serious. He is waiting. The silence is uncomfortable. I shift in my chair and straighten my long skirt, clear my throat.

"Speaking of rules, when I rode in from the airport with Moktar, well, he told me to sit in the front seat. Yet, I saw a sign to the contrary. I was wondering …"

He frowns. "Girls should sit in the back seat. When the driver shifts gears, he could brush his elbow against the girl's breast by accident."

I want to laugh and say something sarcastic, like "Oh thanks, that explains it," but I hold my tongue.

Mr. Al Kahairi begins again. "Next I want to explain the Rules and Customs Enforcement Program. We have three Programs. First, there is the Hospital Security Force. They see to it that patients, visitors, and staff obey the rules. Respect the rules. They police the hospital night and day. Separation of males from females and proper attire are at the top of their list. Some staff violate the rules. The girls, your nurses, talk, joke and laugh with the men. This causes suspicion."

I interrupt him. "Suspicion leads to investigations, investigations are time-consuming, laborious, and inconvenient." A smile and a nod in my direction. He is pleased.

"Then there is the Local Housing Security Program. They patrol the camps on foot as well as in patrol cars—night and day. They watch everyone. It's for everyone's protection. They do not talk to anyone. They do not disturb anyone. They watch—observe. They report what they see—anything suspicious."

I nod, "Suspicion leads to investigation, investigations are time-consuming, laborious, and inconvenient."

"Suspicions are reported to the Royal Commission—the highest level. You will hear ex-pats refer to them as the Authority. Unfortunately, I've picked up that ghastly habit." He laughs heartily, his face pinks up, and he shrugs his shoulders in self-satisfied resignation.

Did he just make an attempt at sounding like a Brit? "You're funny, Mr. Al Kahairi." It dawns on me that this is my first laugh—real laugh —in at least seventy-two hours.

I lean forward, examine the candies on his desk, pick one, unwrap it, place it in my mouth, and allow my taste buds to luxuriate in sugar and peppermint and recall my mother instructing me when I was about five—never take candy from a stranger.

Then Mr. Al Kahairi unwraps a candy, pops it into his mouth. "The Authority is housed in that building over there," he says as he swivels in his chair in the direction of the big picture window.

Talking directly to the back of his head, I say, "in other words, the Authority lives in our backyard." I realize that I just said "our" and a chill runs down my spine. I'm ten million miles from Ashtabula, Ohio.

"Exactly! I don't like it when I get a call from them. When they are informed of rumors, gossip, unpleasant matters, broken rules—and believe me they are," he places his hand on the telephone and pats it, "I get the call. That is why I must be informed of all rumors, rule infractions, unusual goings on, gatherings, suspicious behavior. They will want answers, explanations, solutions to problems, and punishments doled out. So, if you're going to do something that's irregular, if you tell me first, then I can help. If I know in advance then it's easier for me to explain to the Authority."

He stands up. So, I stand up. "If you ever need anything, anything at all, Miss Day, please come to me. Oh, and I have arranged for Moktar to take you back to your apartment. I'm sure it's been a long day for you. See you tomorrow."

. . .

I wince as my elbow brushes against the mildewed and faded green plastic shower curtain. It stinks, too. I dry myself with a rough and ragged brown towel. I want to cry. I am afraid to pull back the spread and see the condition of the bed sheets. I look—nothing crawling. I fall fast asleep.

I'm awakened by a ringing telephone. I feel jumpy. "Hello?"

"Hello, Miss Day, welcome to Yanbu. I am Carolyn Thomas, your neighbor, and a midwife at the hospital. It's lovely that you've arrived." Her voice is music to my ears—a happy tone and a charming British accent. I feel better already.

"Well, thank you. It's very kind of you to call."

"It would be divine if you'd join Jan Hill, she's one of your ER nurses, and me for a cup of coffee."

"I'd love it. But what time is it?"

"It's nearly seven, I believe."

"Day or night?"

"It's Sunday evening. You arrived sometime this morning. You'll be frightfully mixed up for days to come. Don't fret, we've all been through it." She giggles. "We'll pop over to collect you in ten minutes. The way the bloody units are numbered," she giggles again, "you'd never find my place."

"Great, I'll be waiting. And by the way, please call me Kelly." What in God's name am I going to do about the cats? I'll explain about my severe, life-threatening allergy and ask them to shoo the cats away. It'll have to work.

We stroll a very short distance to Carolyn's unit. She's right. With all the units looking alike and no street signs, I would never have been able to find her unit. She lights a cigarette. Carolyn is at least six feet, fleshy, plain featured with huge front teeth and the pale reddish hair I somehow associate with British women. Jan is an African American, about five feet, around one hundred pounds, dainty, cute, and a little sad looking. I'm guessing early forties as I think Carolyn is as well.

Carolyn's unit is identical to the one assigned to me—hideous and dreary. She has appointed it with a truck-load of knickknacks and wall-hangings that give it that "somebody lives here look," although not a pleasing one.

We settle in with our coffee mugs. "Is this your first time in the Kingdom?" Carolyn asks.

"Yes, it is."

"Well, don't judge the Kingdom by this bloody place. I can't believe I've survived it. I spent five years in Jeddah, five years in Riyadh. They were heaven compared to this."

"What do you mean?"

She lights a cigarette, "Don't get me wrong, there are a few decent people around here. Believe me, you'll need them. Most of the bloody staff are incompetent."

"Really?" I look to Jan.

She shakes her head, looks down, and says, "Really, wait until you meet Dr. Small, our medical director."

Carolyn says, "Our idiot pharmacist, Werner, runs out of pain medications among other necessary medications. And, Mr. Al Kahairi, our administrator, well, he's bat-shit crazy. Don't tell me you didn't notice that during your orientation session."

She doesn't wait for a response and starts up again. "Poor Carmencita Banez, the secretary to our hospital pathologist, was jailed for three weeks. They shaved her head and she got flogged every Friday."

"Why? What happened?" I ask.

She lights another cigarette, takes a drag, turns her head, and blows it out slowly. "Because she was found with a man in her apartment. Carmencita and a man, Joel somebody, were just sitting down to a birthday dinner for her when the bloody police knocked on the door. Some bloke phoned the bloody police and squealed on them. Separation of the sexes. It's the law."

"You can't trust anybody around here," Jan says.

"Carmencita, poor thing; cracked up while in jail. She's in our hospital right now waiting to be sent home to the Philippines. That bloody Al Kahairi, will not spend the money on a companion to see that she gets home safely. Instead, they are waiting for the next Filipino nurse to go on leave so that they may use her to escort Carmencita home."

"Nervous breakdowns are very common here," Jan says as Carolyn takes a rare pause. I want to believe that these two women are mere gossips, exaggerating. But a nervous breakdown in this environment is surely believable. On the other hand, it seems that these two characters are trying hard to get me to react. They are mysterious to me, and I am clueless as to their motivation.

"We should tell Kelly about the problem," Jan says in a sad voice as she lowers her head like she is in prayer. "She's going to find out eventually. Somebody will tell her." She shrugs her narrow shoulders.

Carolyn lights another cigarette, sighs, and begins another tale. "My apartment was broken into, and I was robbed. This happened some six weeks ago. Some bloody nut came in through the sliding glass doors. Most glass doors in the units are ill-fitting. By the way, you should put your sofa against the patio doors just to be safe. About a thousand riyals, and lots of jewelry were taken."

"That's awful. Who would do this to you?"

"Don't know. I've got a reputation for buying lots of gold jewelry, I know that."

I look down at my hands and see that I've ripped up three cuticles.

"My contract expires at the end of the month, and I'll be home in Ipswich soon if things go smoothly. I hope my smoking doesn't bother you. I'm a chain smoker."

"What's the problem?" I ask.

"Al Kahairi is holding up my clearance papers so I can't exit the Kingdom. He's saying I gave a false report to Security. The hospital is short of mid-wives and I think that's why my papers are being held up." She lets out a groan.

"I've met all my financial objectives. I put a large deposit on a lovely cottage in the Cotswolds, purchased a car, and I'm taking my family to Barcelona on a holiday." She throws her hands up in a grand gesture.

"I'm impressed."

"I'm not sure I'll know how to carry on when I return to the civilized world. You're a little crazy after this place. You can't even tell your family and friends about this bloody place. They'd never believe you. Pardon me while I head for the loo."

"I don't tell my family any of this either. They wouldn't believe it." Jan says. She is as sober as Carolyn is high.

I look at my watch. I've only been with these two women a short while but it seems like an eternity. "It sounds like this is a very stressful place to live and work."

"All the nurses suffer from insomnia, myself included."

"Tell me about yourself, Jan."

She clears her throat. "I'm from Detroit. I am a trauma nurse specialist." She is soft-spoken and serious. "I've been here eighteen months now, I guess. You lose track of time here. The monotony can do that to you."

"Monotony? Incompetent staff, a house robbery, flogging and nervous breakdowns. Really?"

Nonplussed by my implied accusation of fabrication, Carolyn jumps in. "It's not so bad here. You get used to it. You can make your own fun. How did you happen to come here?"

"To answer your question, I responded to an ad in the Sunday paper. I need to be going now. It was nice of you to call and invite me for coffee." I think these two women are odd.

"Don't go. It's early. I'll brew another pot of coffee and we'll have some biscuits," says Carolyn.

"No, I really must go." Any more time with them and I'll be frightfully mixed up for life.

On our walk to 5350, I say, "I understand the basic rules for females are: don't wear figure revealing clothes; don't show skin (arms or legs); don't mingle with men, and don't drink alcohol. Is there anything the recruiter left out?"

"If it were only that simple," says the quiet one. "It's hard to explain. You'll see for yourself. There are so many double-standards here. And the rules are not enforced consistently and they vary throughout the regions. What flies in one area doesn't in another."

"They are bloody two-faced hypocrites. They're paranoid and sex crazy too," says Carolyn.

"Is it that bad?" I ask with a hint of amusement. Hopefully, it's just their unique perception of things.

"Saudi men think that all Western women are decadent whores and that we are trying to seduce them. Wait until you see how they look at you. They ogle your boobs," Carolyn says.

"Do some women get involved with Saudi men?"

"Yes, and it's bloody dangerous. Once he has you, he'll blackmail you and tell you that you must be with his friends. There is no turning back. No woman wants to be stoned to death."

"Wow, this really gets complicated, doesn't it?"

"It bloody well does and by the way, Al Kahairi has two wives. Watch out for him. If he doesn't like you, you're in trouble. He will have his spies throughout the hospital reporting to him on your every move."

I've got a headache now and I remind them of my allergy. We turn our first corner and a scrawny brown cat crosses our path. I jump and grab Jan's arm. Carolyn stamps her feet, waves her arms, shouting, "Shoo, shoo." Then she giggles. I feel like a jerk.

Then on our third turn in the housing maze a sizeable brown cat slips out from under a courtyard gate. "Oh shit!" I scream.

"It's okay, Kelly—he's gone already," says Jan.

Carolyn is laughing hysterically.

We're at my front door, and Jan volunteers to come in and show me where the emergency telephone numbers are posted on the kitchen wall. "Just in case."

"I'll find them. Goodnight, you two."

I snap the lock on the door, check to be sure the windows and the sliding glass doors are shut tight. I'm going to get out of this insane place. I need my passport. How do I get it back? The hell with the contract. I need an airline ticket out of here. How would I get to the airport? I pace from room to room. I feel so alone and intimidated. I feel like Carolyn and Jan are trying to make me feel unsafe. A shower will help. I will get myself together. What am I going to do about the cats? I've been scared to death of cats since I can remember.

This place is dangerous—both physically and psychologically. Already I feel a little crazy—paranoid: the two women with the stories, the emergency phone numbers, Mr. Al Kahairi, the twenty pictures, mysterious Moktar, and all the stuff that happened in the Jeddah Airport.

If I can get some sleep, I'll think better tomorrow. I won't panic. My eyelids are heavy—I'm exhausted. What a rotten start to a new adventure. This is hell.

Chapter 2

Saturday, September 12, 1987

"Allahu Akbar," a solemn male voice intones a prayer in Arabic that is intended for everyone's edification. I make a note of it in my diary. I want to capture every detail of my adventure. The woman seated next to me says in a British accent, "Do you know what he's saying?"

"No, I don't. Do you?"

"God is Great," she says with a flash of amusement in her eyes. "Get used to it. You'll hear that five times a day."

I want to engage her in conversation but she pulls a blanket over her shoulders and shifts her body into a "do not disturb please" position. I must have "novice expatriate" stamped on my forehead.

The jumbo jet takes off on time from Barajas International Airport in Madrid. The large crowd of passengers is given the routine safety instructions in three different languages. A brief glance to my right and my left tells me that three languages won't cover all the bases. We look like a delegation to a world congress. There are both hatless men and women in designer jeans and Reeboks as well as turbaned men and women in colorful flowing garments and sandals. I'm fascinated by what I see and hear: an infinite variety of clothing, beautiful shades of skin, and that marvelously rich and diverse human thing called language. The man next to me calls the flight attendant "love" and I hear her say "gracias" to the woman across the aisle. I hear voices from men's throats that I can't imitate. I feel high.

Today is my thirtieth birthday. I feel as though I'm sixteen—excited to the brim. From Ashtabula to Cleveland to New York to Madrid—I'm almost there.

A one-hour stop in Rome, where we are not permitted to deplane, is followed by lunch service, catered by Marriott. No alcoholic beverages are offered, but a glass of water is served to each passenger. I'm enjoying the standard airline food as I try to imagine how my first work experience in an exotic and ancient culture ten thousand miles from my home in Ashtabula, Ohio will unfold.

At last, the usual announcement about tray tables and seats in the upright position in preparation for landing is made. I've got goose bumps.

Wow, I'm amazed. This airport is gigantic. I don't know what I expected but I didn't expect this. It's ultra modern, sleek, and spacious. Computers are everywhere. All the signs are in the beautiful cursive Arabic script and the plain but familiar Roman alphabet spells English words. An enormous Welcome to King Abdul Aziz International Airport illuminated sign makes me smile. My heart is beating fast. I did it. I'm here in Jeddah, Saudi Arabia with one short flight left on this long journey. I'm both tired and energized.

At the passport check-in counter, a dark-skinned young man in a neatly pressed khaki uniform stares at a computer screen for a long time, then he takes my passport and ticket and tells me to have a seat in the Transit Passenger Area just a few steps away. I check my watch; twenty-five minutes until my next flight which is due to depart at 4 p.m. After a short while a man in a crisp white shirt and perfectly straight black neck tie escorts me and two other women to the baggage claim area.

An Irish brogue breaks the silence as we wait for our luggage. "The men are good looking, aren't they?" says the pretty brunette with eyes bluer than a Monet painting.

"Indeed, they are." I smile.

When each of us has all of our luggage, he shepherds us to customs. I prefer to do things for myself. I find his assistance unnecessary.

Next, a portly and not-so-tidy old man in a hunter green open-neck shirt and matching trousers indicates with a nod of his balding head for me to open my big suitcase. Without a word, I comply. His large gloved hands dig into carefully packed skirts, blouses, bras, panties, jeans, a pair of white sneakers, reading material, and, a see-through cosmetic bag which includes several tampons. His search for prohibited and restricted goods is thorough. I know I didn't bring with me weapons, drugs, alcohol or what might be considered pornographic literature, either printed or recorded on video. Nonetheless, all three back issues of Newsweek are confiscated. I read in the survival handbook what might be considered pornographic or objectionable to the Islamic religion or Muslim customs may be confiscated. Then this old man who handled my personal property affixes a small orange sticker to my suitcase.

Only five minutes are left until take off. Our escort, who speaks English very well, resumes his duties and gives simple and direct commands in a monotone. I am told, "Wait here." Then the other women, nurses from County Cork, Ireland, en route to Tabuk disappear under his command.

Doing as I'm told, I wait to the right of a short line of travelers checking their bags. Acutely aware that time is passing, I desperately want to move things along. I glance at my watch. My flight is due to take off now. I see the escort, easily recognized by his white shirt and straight black tie, coming toward me. I step forward to greet him. "Sir, my flight should be departing now." He steps to the desk and confers in Arabic. Returning to me he says, "Miss, flight 110 has just departed."

"I can't believe this! What time is the next flight?"

"Not until tomorrow. Tonight you will be put up in a hotel and you'll leave in the morning for Yanbu. Please have a seat in the Transit Passenger Area."

Is this the protection of females that I read about? I feel demeaned by their we're in charge of you, little girl attitude.

A long half hour passes—I return to the check-in desk. "Would you please give me some information? I missed my flight, and I want to know who is supposed to be making hotel arrangements for me. Who is in charge here?"

"You must speak to the supervisor, over there."

Aware of my impatience and irritability, I change my tone and say, "Thank you, sir," and force a smile.

The supervisor, a well-groomed Saudi Airline employee, fluent in English, says, "You will not be going to a hotel. You must stay in the Transit Passenger Area tonight."

"But Sir, your staff promised me a hotel room, you caused me to miss my flight, and now I'm stuck in a waiting area until morning! What's going on here?"

His eyes avoid mine as he gives this explanation: "You cannot leave the airport without your sponsor or a representative from your employer. Furthermore, women may not rent hotel rooms. This is our custom."

I can tell this isn't the first time he's given that speech. "Where's my passport and my ticket?" I glare at him.

He remains composed and says, "They are being held at the Security Desk in the Transit Passenger Area." His pleasing physical appearance and his composed behavior are in sharp contrast to me, an unravelling hag with a mouth full of germs and a short temper.

Well what did you expect?—a voice inside me says. You heard that women are treated as children. You read about strange customs and lots of regulations. You said you could live in a foreign culture for an entire year. I tell the voice to shut up.

I sink into a black vinyl chair that shares its arms with two other chairs. About thirty feet in front of me is a large grey steel desk surrounded by a handful of security guys who smoke, laugh, tell stories, and come and go at intervals. This crew is holding my airline ticket and precious passport hostage. I feel like a little girl who is wearing a large tag strung around her neck, travelling from LA to visit Daddy who divorced Mommy and is now living with his girlfriend in New

York City. After a while, I get up to stretch my legs and relocate to the next section for a change of scene.

"Where are you going?" shouts a security guy in a stern voice. I stop in my tracks and turn towards him. His walk is slow and deliberate. My stomach muscles tighten and my breathing increases. Now standing closer than I think he should, I take a step back. He's tall and bulky with huge brown eyes and a big nose.

"I want to sit over there." I point.

"Sit over here!" he commands and points to my original seat. I mumble, " bastard" under my breath and truck back to where I started out. I don't want a hassle, I rationalize. Why argue with that self-important bully? In full view of each other, I watch him. He talks fast, laughs loudly, moves decisively. I label him Tough Guy.

It's going to be a long night. As far as I can see, I am the only person—let alone female—in this area with these security guys who seem more relaxed by the hour. Airport traffic has come to a stop. I get up from my uncomfortable chair and walk towards Tough Guy and his crew. Tough Guy gets up from his chair and again starts his slow and deliberate walk towards me. I believe he is showing off for his peers.

"Where may I get a cup of coffee, sir?"

He doesn't hesitate. "You must wait here for five minutes. I'll let you know when you can go upstairs." His haughty grin makes me cringe. I believe he's enjoying this.

Fifteen minutes, maybe twenty, pass. Changing his strategy, Tough Guy, while remaining seated at his steel desk, shouts to me, "You can go, but you must return in one hour." He checks his watch then says, "No, no, you must return in thirty minutes."

"All right, sir." How odd that he needs to rule over me in this way. Is he afraid of me? The other men seemed to be just following rules.

As I reach the escalator, I am directed to a search booth. A stout woman shrouded in black, hair completely covered with a veil concealing all but her thick eyebrows and dark eyes outlined in black, brushes my torso with an electronic scanning device. This is my first encounter with a Saudi woman and I'm not even sure if she is a Saudi. In any case, she is tucked away in a poorly lit search booth in the Jeddah International Airport. Unlike the security guys, she is covered, silent, and hidden. I'm curious about her so I smile and say, "hello." She doesn't smile back or answer me. Instead, she turns away from me. I'm disappointed. It's just the two of us. No one would know if she made eye contact and smiled. What does she think of me? How did she get her job? How does she react to Tough Guy? I'm itching to get to the nitty-gritty of my adventure. Patience—I've got an entire year. I'll observe for now. Ten thousand tough guys aren't going to stop me.

I ride a steep escalator to the great hall of airport shops. Fancy telephones, perfumes, toys and Ponds Cold Cream are yours for the asking price in Saudi halalahs and riyals when the shops are open. I'm the only window shopper. I see a clerk at a snack bar at the far end of this great hall. I approach the counter. "Do you speak English?"

"Yes, mom."

I recognize he is a Filipino and my comfort level rises. "Cumstaka," I greet him.

"Ma buta," he replies with an enormous grin. "You speak Tagalog?"

"You've just heard all the Tagalog I know. May I have a cup of coffee? How much? Do you take U.S. dollars?"

"Sorry mom, no."

"Where can I exchange some money?"

Sorry mom, no place here." I stand at the counter and glare at him as though it was his fault.

He pushes a paper cup of steaming black coffee into my hand.

"Thank you. I'm really grateful for your kindness." I take a sip of the hot coffee and rest my elbows on the counter. "This is a difficult place, isn't it?"

As though he didn't hear me, he starts asking questions. "Are you a nurse, mom? Are you from the United States, mom? Where in the United States, mom?"

"Ashtabula, Ohio." He looks perplexed but doesn't speak. That was a conversation stopper.

I look directly into his sad brown eyes, "You didn't answer my question."

"Well mom, it's difficult. But you're an American. It'll be easier for you."

His comment makes me feel sad. "How have you been treated?" He lowers his brown eyes, looks into the steel sink below the counter, and plucks a large, crude, yellow sponge from the surface of the grayish brown dishwater, squeezes it with all his might, and says, "Don't get me wrong, you'll be fine. I shouldn't have said that." He sponges the countertop directly in front of me, then flings the sponge into a slop bucket that sits on the floor in a corner along with a mop. "Really, you'll be fine. Good night, mom."

I head for the down escalator. As I near it, a puny young man in a sky blue uniform with white trim and pants inches above his shoe tops, steps up and shouts at me "la la la." His body language supports my hunch that "la" means no.

"What? I can't go down the escalator?" He continues to yell, "la la la" while waving his arms. He reaches the escalator, bends down, flips a switch and the moving steps come to a halt. Another guy trying to take charge of me. "La, yourself," I yell then dart down the remaining steps of the escalator, run around a corner, slip past the ladies search booth, and return to the Transit Passenger Area.

I pace the area to rid myself of a cramp in the arch of my left foot as Saturday evening ends and Sunday begins. Tough Guy approaches, but now smiling warmly. I hope he is pleased, I've returned within the thirty minute window. Making good eye contact, he asks with interest, "Where are you from?"

I doubt that he's heard of Ashtabula, Ohio, so I say, "The United States of America."

"Are you a teacher?" His eyes locked on mine.

"No, I'm a nurse."

"Where are you going?" He conducts his interview in good English with a heavy Arabic accent and perpetual grin. His age is around thirty.

"Yanbu."

"I know that. Where will you work?"

"At a hospital."

"Is this your first time here?"

"Yes, it is."

"Do you have any children?"

"No, I don't have any children. Do you?"

"Do you have a husband?"

"I'm not married. Are you?"

"I'm asking the questions. Do you like to drink alcohol and dance?"

"What do you want from me? You aren't supposed to be asking me these questions."

His manner becomes truculent. "You are supposed to be in the Women's Room."

"What?"

"Yes, whenever you get to an airport, the first thing you should do is find out where the Women's Room is. That's the first thing you should do." His deep voice is louder and more adamant now, and his right arm is signaling the way. "I will show you."

"I don't need the Women's Room," I snap. I'm curious. Why am I the only female passenger around here? I follow him. He leads me to a dark brown curtain that drapes an entrance way. He pulls the heavy curtain back with his right hand and with his left he motions for me to enter a small, dark, stuffy vestibule that cannot be more than three by five feet. He reeks of cigarette smoke. His breathing is hard with a whistling breathy sound like an asmathic's. He coughs a short, tight cough. Now's not the time for me to lecture him on the health hazards of cigarette smoking. He directs me to go left around a contrived partition but doesn't accompany me.

There before me are about a dozen women, a handful of children, and a few infants curled up on canvas cots. There are a few women with children sprawled out on the floor on makeshift mats. Some are sleeping; others are tossing restlessly. Pairs of eyes examine me. I feel like an intruder. I am the only white face and Western dressed woman in this stuffy and drab holding station. It's quiet, except for the rustling of clothing and blankets. I feel like my five-foot two-inch frame is towering over a special gathering to which I was not invited. Are they holing up in the Women's Room because they can't rent hotel rooms without being accompanied by their husbands or fathers? Where are the husbands? Can they even travel without their husbands? Now's not the time to ask: does anyone here speak English and would you mind terribly if I asked you a few questions?

I self-consciously return to the vestibule where Tough Guy waits for me.

"You should stay there," he commands.

"No, I won't stay in that stuffy room. Is this the best you can do for women and children?" As I turn to exit, his thick beige fingers seductively brush my ear and cheek—my eyes widen, my mouth flies open. His big brown eyes look wild. He scares me. My heart pounding, I storm out of the vestibule.

I plunk into a chair in the Transit Passenger Area. I'm weary. The hands on my watch hover around 4 a.m. I try to doze off but I can't. I'm restless.

Voices on my right draw my attention. A man in his fifties and a boy probably in his late teens settle in with hand luggage about fifteen seats away from me. I decide to distract myself from ruminating about all the nonsense that has happened in this crazy airport tonight and walk over to them. I've gained courage from the fact that Tough Guy has decided to leave me alone, at least for now. The lean figure of the adolescent appears rigid, his face fixed in a painful grimace, while the older man holds him in a fatherly embrace. I say "hello" and slip into the seat next to the father. Communication among us doesn't flow easily.

They tell me they are from Greece. They guessed I'm an American. I gather that there is a problem with the son's work visa. The son has worked as a laborer in Saudi Arabia for two years. He was unaware of a problem with his visa as he reentered the Kingdom from his visit home. He is being detained until his sponsor (employer) shows up and straightens the matter out. Two years in the Kingdom makes him at least twenty but he appears so young, and so frightened—emotionally broken. The dad—so terribly worried and tense. The son cries. I feel sorry for them. Tough Guy watches us from the desk but doesn't come near us.

The worried dad excuses himself and heads for the escalator. I make feeble attempts at small talk with the young man. He owns more English words than his dad. He and his dad work at the same place. The dad returns with three cups of coffee and hands me one of them. I'm touched by his thoughtfulness and thank him. He repeats "you're welcome" several times as tension leaves his face. We sip our coffee in silence. Then I make an awkward attempt to comfort them by saying, "I know things will work out."

With an ache between my shoulder blades, I retreat to my assigned area and start to worry about not only them, but me as well. Not in possession of either my airline ticket nor my precious passport, I sip on my second cup of strong black coffee given to me by strangers.

It's around 5 a.m. and the dad and son are being escorted away. The dad looks over his shoulder at me and nods farewell as his son clings to his side. I have a sick feeling in the pit of my stomach.

Over a loud speaker a deep male voice startles me as he intones the "call to prayer." The guys over at the security desk disappear except for Tough Guy. It's just the two of us now. He gets up from behind his steel desk and starts that same slow and deliberate walk towards me. But somehow it feels a hundred times more menacing this time. My hands grasp tightly on the arms of the chair. He stops smack in front of me with the tips of his shoes no more than inches from mine. I feel trapped, small, and scared to death. If I push myself up, our bodies will be touching. It's like in a dream when you try to scream but can't. Nothing comes out. He reaches down and grabs my left wrist.

Jesus Christ, I'm losing it! What in God's name did I just do? My feet are propelling my body through space as though I'm weightless. What's happening to me? I couldn't have done that—I'm not a violent person. I've never, ever in my entire life struck anyone. The palm of my hand is burning. My legs stop moving. I stand before a little sink, turn on the ice cold water and let it run all over the burning, red and swollen hand that I can't believe belongs to me. Without touching or drying my hand, I drag myself into a toilet stall, slide the lock with my left hand, sit on the toilet, sweat, and cry.

What will happen next? Will I be arrested, carried off to jail, interrogated, given a chance to explain my actions? I committed an act of violence. My right hand is the evidence. I didn't plan to do it. I didn't mean to do it. It just happened. I'll deny the action. His word against mine—no witnesses—no witnesses? Yes, yes, I'm sure no witnesses.

I'll stay right here and hide until my flight is due to depart. Please God, nobody comes for me.

I return to the sink and splash cold water on my face, swallow water from the cup of my hand, comb my hair with my fingers, and vomit coffee-colored gastric acids into the little sink.

I'm weak and slide to the cold floor, my legs and feet straight out in front of me. I lean against the wall. I summon the courage to examine and compare hands. Both palms are a little wide, my fingers bear no rings, are not long and slender but acceptably delicate and feminine—distinctively unweaponlike. The right hand remains swollen and red.

I pull my diary from my big, black, carry-on tote. I hold the eight by six inch cloth-bound book in my left hand. I rest my swollen right hand on the soft cover with its gentle design of silver foliage and pale peach poppies.

Aunt Mary Sheila, my favorite aunt, gave me this going away gift as a symbol of her silent support of my adventure. On the inside of the front cover, she neatly printed, in its entirety, my favorite poem, Crossing Ohio When Poppies Bloom in Ashtabula by Carl Sandburg. She was my mother's younger sister by thirteen years. She spent most of her adult years as a Catholic nun teaching grade school in an orphanage in Dublin, Ireland. On the heels of Vatican II, she returned to secular life and moved back home to Ashtabula. She died of ovarian cancer. We buried her three days before I embarked on this adventure.

I read the poem, cry, wipe my tears with my sleeve. Turn to my first entry and begin to retrace my steps in search of clues that might have led up to my first—and please God—only violent act of my life. I didn't hit him for nothing.

. . .

It's 7:30 a.m. I jam my diary back into the tote. I leave this little washroom where I've spent the last few hours and head straight to the airline counter. A male Saudi Airline employee leads me to the domestic boarding area. This meticulously groomed and polite man calls me "Kelly" and without blinking an eye says, "I will turn your passport over to the steward onboard the aircraft, he will hand it over to the authorities at the Yanbu airport and they will give it to your sponsor. This is our custom." I feel like a prisoner and I'm scared. The long climb up the portable steps to the aircraft pains my thighs.

I came here to make money. I was pink-slipped back at Ashtabula General Hospital, on July 28. I answered an ad in the Sunday paper. Telephone interviews with Sammy Samuels, a head hunter with an international recruitment firm based in Moses Lake, Washington, were conducted. Offer extended. Offer hastily and without thoughtful consideration accepted. I rushed to the passport office and I rushed to the nearest clinic to have an AIDS test done. A negative result is a prerequisite for the job. But what have I gotten myself into? Just yesterday I was so confident in myself and my decision to come all this way to live and work in an ancient culture. My parents and relatives—dead set against this decision and my friends—all of them, leery. Only my now deceased Aunt Sheila Mary supported my decision. I will make this work.

Chapter 3

Monday, September 14, 1987

Fidelis and I walk to the hospital under the burning sun. A thick layer of sunscreen covers my face and throat. I ask Fidelis about the crazy stuff Carolyn told me. She says there is usually a kernel of truth in the wild stories. People do exaggerate, even lie, of course, and over time stories get bigger and more fantastic each time they're told. She supports Carolyn's and Jan's assertions that the enforcement of rules and customs vary widely throughout the Kingdom, the mixed bag of double standards, who gets away with what, and the uneven manner with which infractions, violations, and suspicious behavior are dealt with. Fidelis doesn't deny or confirm any of the stories. She makes no comment on the storytellers or the villains in the stories.

"Loneliness can lead to actions that otherwise might not have been taken, and loneliness is a daily battle for some," Fidelis cautions.

I go straight to my office, unlock the door, put my purse in the bottom desk drawer and before I can sit down the phone rings. I pick up and hear an American male voice.

"Miss Day, I heard you just arrived. Oh, I'm Dr. Small. Please come to my office. I'm just down the hall from you. Turn left, no, I mean right." He chuckles.

"I'm eager to meet you. I'll be right there."

At last a fellow American—someone I can, hopefully, have a sane conversation with. Get some perspective on all this. I could use a good friend.

"You must be Dr. Small." I extend my hand. He shakes it. He has a sweaty palm. "I'm Kelly Day, director of nursing." I smell orange peels.

"Welcome. Well, how are things so far?" He laughs.

"It's been interesting. I had an orientation session yesterday with Mr. Al Kahairi on rules and things. With jet lag and all, I feel disoriented and uncomfortable. I don't have my passport in my possession. I'm finding this place intimidating—disconcerting with all the stories I'm hearing."

Dr. Small looks confused. Doesn't he find this place strange? He tugs at his ear and scales of dry skin fall on his shoulder and trickle down to the lapel of his white lab coat. It's disgusting. I grit my teeth and stare into his anxious green eyes. "Do you know what I mean?"

"Oh please, excuse my manners. Have a seat." He points to a conference table and chairs. Orange peels, both old and fresh, are scattered on the table top along with a used paper napkin and a pen knife. He makes no excuses for the mess. He looks like no one I've ever met. His face is shaped like a diamond. His complexion is pale. His hair is straight, sandy with grey temples. His height is five-five, tops.

I try again. "This place is strange." I pause. "Intimidating."

"It's different, I'll say that." Nervous laughter accompanies yet another tug of his ear and the white medical coat is dusted again with dead skin. "My wife should arrive in four weeks or so, if things go all right. We've been married thirty-three years and the Saudis are insisting that we produce the original marriage certificate. We've been working on this for six months, I think. I don't know, we've moved so many times. I've worked in the Kingdom in the past, about ten years ago. I'm here since March first and I'm still adjusting, I guess."

He pauses, jumps up, walks around the office like he's searching for something. "Oh, by the way, all new hires have a one-time opportunity to call home on the international line here in my office. Would you like to call now?" He studies his watch. "It's late evening in the Midwest, I think." He informs me that it's a three minute call. "I have the international code and directions here somewhere." He shifts manila folders from one side of the desk to the other, knocks over an empty pencil holder, discovers a photo of his deceased dog under a stack of unopened mail, finds a toothbrush that he's been looking for, along with band-aids, but no international telephone code. Then he checks his wallet. No luck.

I pass on the three minute free phone call. I'm afraid I'll burst into tears: beg and plead with my parents to call the State Department to get me the hell out of here. I guess that I won't be leaning on Dr. Small, my fellow American, for support.

His phone rings, he grimaces, picks it up and says, "Yes, Mr. Al Kahairi, she's right here—I'll send her right over." He raises his eyebrows, "Better go, he wants to see you now."

I stop at my office and take a few minutes to reflect. I'm uneasy here but I want to stick around to see what happens. In the words of Dr. Small—it's different—I'll say that. I want to put the picture together or at least fill in some of the gaps. I want to stay with this adventure. I'm thirty. It's time to expand my horizons. Now, on to Mr. Al Kahairi's office.

"Good morning, Mr. Al Kahairi."

"Good morning, Miss Day. Have a seat please. You had a good night's rest?"

"Yes, I did." It's none of his business that I tossed and turned and ruminated until 2:00 a.m. about my decision to take this adventure a million miles from Ashtabula in the face of objections by family and friends.

He heaves a sigh, his eyebrows pull together, the corners of his mouth drop down and disappear into fleshy jowls. "This place is like a small town. There isn't much to do here. There is lots of gossip. Lots of gossip. You will hear many stories, many lies."

"I'm glad you brought that up. I've been inundated with a host of … ah … stories. Well, I … ah … wondered about Carolyn's apartment theft, and her concerns about a problem surrounding her leaving here."

"Carolyn is a liar and a trouble maker! There was no theft. No evidence. She filed false reports. She called her embassy about this matter. That was suspicious. If she was not guilty, why did she do that? Because of the false reports she must be cleared by the Authority before she exits the Kingdom and this red tape is what Carolyn is calling the problem. She has caused the problem." He opens his desk drawer, pulls out a hand full of individually wrapped hard candies and tosses them on his desk. "Help yourself."

I take one as instructed—glad to fill the silent space with the task of unwrapping the candy. I take my time with it.

A smirk spreads across his broad, fat face. "Miss Day, I fixed your Igama problem. Moktar will drive you to town to have your picture taken. Bring back twenty, please. He will pick you up here at the hospital promptly after the noon prayer. Sit in the back seat."

He rises from his chair. I rise from mine. He points to the candy and says, "Take them with you. They're good, aren't they?"

I grab a few candies and return to my office, slump in my chair, and admit to myself that King Khaled, as Carolyn calls him, intimidates me. He is totally outrageous, funny, and has two wives. I stare out the window. What did I get myself into? Rumors? Lies? Suspicions? What do you have if you don't have trust? What about all this control? I have a great big headache.

A fair-haired and roly-poly gentleman, probably in his early forties and dressed in a green surgical scrub suit, stands in my doorway clearing his throat, obviously to get my attention.

"Hello." I stand up and greet him. Without a word he presents me with a white paper bag.

"For me?"

With mischief in his huge blue eyes and with a chipper English accent he says, "Welcome to the Magic Kingdom, as you Americans always say."

I chuckle and open the bag—coffee and a donut. "This donut smells good and looks delicious. Please share it with me."

"If you insist, Miss Day. I'd never argue with my boss. I'm Steve Luney, your ER manager."

Over coffee and a shared cream-filled chocolate donut, which serves as my lunch, he tells me with a joke.

"The big dumb blonde from Brighton Beach went to the doctor and asked to be put on a diet. The doctor recommended that she eat regularly for two days then skip a day then eat regularly for two more days then skip a day and return to him the following day. He estimated that she'd drop about a half a stone. She returned as instructed and she had lost an entire stone. "Did you follow my instructions?" the doctor asked.

"Yes, I tell you though, I thought I was going to drop dead on the third day."

"From hunger, you mean?"

"No, from skipping," she replied.

I feign laughter.

Then he launches into a run-down on the emergency room activities, and I learn his job also includes overseeing the switchboard, scheduling the translators, and running the men's ward.

Without any prompting, Steve tells me about himself. "I'm a licensed nurse from East Sussex, England—close to Brighton Beach. I came here after working three years in Jeddah at a much bigger hospital—my contract ran out. Where I was awfully happy, I might add. I've been in Yanbu three months now, and I detest this ghastly town. I have nine months left on my contract. I can't wait to get out of here. But enough about me. How was your trip—all the way from Ohio? Any problems?"

"No. Not really. You know I'm from Ohio?"

"Word gets out about everybody—you'll see. I always find the Jeddah Airport a bit tiresome. I hear Western women complain about it all the time."

"Take me on a tour." He springs from his chair and leads me down a hallway.

"Let's kick off the Grand Tour in the Main Lobby, which I prefer to call the Great Hall. You will please note the frightfully larger than life oil paintings of King Fahd, the Custodian of the Two Holy Mosques and his predecessors." He tilts his head towards the paintings and rolls his big blue eyes. "No queens among them and no pun intended."

My introduction to the staff is haphazard and doesn't take long. Everyone is cordial. Many seem surprised when I extend my hand. The bedside nurses are from the Philippines and the head nurses are from Western Europe, mostly Great Britain. Housekeeping and various other less skilled departments are staffed by Sri Lankans, Bangladeshians, and Sudanese, among many other nationalities. East Indians, Pakistanis, Egyptians, and Lebanese are among the professional and semi-professional staff.

In my wildest dreams, I never thought I would meet anyone from Sri Lanka. Steve introduces me to Sunil. He's a handsome young Sinhalese with a bright smile. He's wearing a short white lab coat over a solid brown T-shirt and, from his waist to mid-calf he is wrapped in a cloth of colorful geometric designs. He works as a technician in the blood lab. As we stroll towards the women's unit, Steve tells me that Sunil was weary of fighting the Tamil Tigers and sought refuge here.

Without a pause, Steve jumps to another subject. "We have twenty-five female beds on this unit. We see mostly routine cases: pneumonia, gastritis, heart problems, gallbladder disease and backaches. Many of the patients are malingerers—most of them 'backaches.' They like their medications. As you can see, many are sleeping. The Saudis are nocturnal. They come alive after supper."

"Steve, tell me about the malingering."

While Steve is running on about malingering, my mind returns to his comment about Western women and the Jeddah International Airport. On one hand, I'd like to pursue that comment with him, but on the other hand I wouldn't want to inadvertently or maybe impulsively tell a stranger about my behavior in that airport.

"The women are bored at home. They are house-bound, you know. The hospital serves as a social center for them, and consequently, they make unnecessary visits to the ER and then they have a grand time visiting in the women's waiting room. The Saudi men are malingerers, too. They want to be excused from work. They are very demanding, rude and uncouth—uncivilized, really—awfully bad mannered. You wouldn't dare talk back to one of them because they'll complain to Mr. Al Kahairi and a report will be made. You could have money deducted from your paycheck as a result of a Saudi complaining about you."

"Steve, you're kidding—money deducted—really?"

"They do whatever they want to us. Be thankful you're a Westerner. They're much harder on the Asians, especially the Filipinos."

I'm stunned as we pass Saudi women in the corridors of the outpatient clinics. They look like moving, faceless black statues. Not surprising, they're shrouded in black, but what strikes me is that their faces are completely covered with a heavy black veil. Not even their eyes are exposed. Some even wear black gloves. Their shoes are a mixture of styles and colors from bright red spike high heels to plain white flats. Obviously, they can see through the heavy veil because they aren't walking into walls. I don't like that they can see my face and I can't see theirs.

"Have they scheduled your inventory yet?" Steve asks as we head back to my office.

"No, what's that about?"

"They inventory every bloody thing in your apartment. All furnishings—even down to the teaspoons. Make sure you get a signed copy of the bloody thing. Check it carefully. If they determine something is missing when you're ready to leave the Kingdom, they'll charge you an astronomical price for it. Fidelis Martinez does the inventory. She is a spy for King Khaled and none of the Filipino nurses like her—one of their very own."

"Right now that's the least of my concerns." More stories, I'm sick of it already.

"Oh, and by the way, I recommend dining at the Big Bun in the mall. It's one of the two options available. The other is the Pizza Palace which is revolting."

Thankfully, Moktar interrupts our meeting and orders me to follow him as he is now ready to whisk me to town. I climb in the backseat. The photo shoot was uncomplicated. I expected to be asked a lot of questions or to sign a thousand papers or something. I guess Mr. Al Kahairi did "fix the problem" like he said, he did. I can understand why expats get confused. You expect one thing and you get another.

I have a real conversation with Moktar on the way back to the hospital. He's got a wife, three little kids, prays five times a day, does the grocery shopping for the family, has ambitions beyond his current job.

He sounds proud and enthusiastic as he explains, "There are about two million foreign workers in the Kingdom. We want to become self-sufficient—run things for ourselves. Expand health care and education, create a sound infrastructure—like electricity and telecommunications—things like that. I want to be an active part in all of this—move up the ladder as they say." He smiles.

"But doesn't it get complicated—depending on others, many of whom have behaviors that are often disagreeable to the host country?"

"It does. The more we know about Western ways, observe them, try to explain to our wives and children ..." his voice trails off. Then says, "Allah takes care of everything."

. . .

I make my way to Fidelis' office. Her office, if you can call it that, is situated in the same area as the industrial sized washers, dryers, and mangler. Her alcove looks like a large cleaning supply cupboard. She sits behind a small desk looking very executive-like studying what appears to be a supply catalogue.

I raise my voice above the laundry room noise. "Hello." I've startled her.

"You found me."

"It wasn't easy. What smells so good? What is it?" I walk a few steps to the crowded shelves of cleaning rags, plastic trash bags, mop heads, gallon jugs of bleach, furniture polish, and soap.

Fidelis says, "Keep walking."

I bump into a cleaning cart on wheels with its buckets of soapy water and rinse water. I take a deep breath in through my nostrils and let it out slowly. "It's the soapy water. What makes it smell so good?"

"Lemongrass is one of the ingredients in that brand of vegetable oil soap. That's why I order it. But what I like is …" she gets up from her desk, takes a cloth from a shelf and a squirt bottle filled with an orange liquid. She squirts the solution on to the cloth, takes a whiff and hands the cloth to me.

"Orange peel in furniture polish. I have to special order it," she says with pride.

I laugh and tell her about the orange peels on the table in Dr. Small's office.

"Let's get out of here, Fidelis, before we both get high on cleaning supplies." I tell her I need her to walk to and from work with me, at least until I get the cat problem solved, which I haven't a clue how to solve. "I can manage the broad streets, but it's stepping into the Camp Five maze and the small courtyard at the entrance to 5350 that's my biggest challenge."

"No problem, Kelly."

We walk in the miserable heat.

"Do you want to go through the inventory with me?" she asks as we enter 5350.

"No, thank you." I sit on the ugly black couch with the cigarette burns while she moves about the dump counting tables, chairs, chipped dishes, torn pillow slips and bent teaspoons—everything. I dislike the implication that I could be a thief. Maybe they've dealt with a lot of thieves. After all, Carolyn claims she was robbed. I sign without reading the ten pages or so document she puts in front of me, and I don't ask for a copy.

"I'm sorry if I appear rude—I know you're just doing your job. It's just that this little unit disgusts me. It's so shabby and ugly."

"Not everyone would agree with you. For some, it's a big apartment —and not really shabby. I don't know why you're here. For many of us it is strictly economics, and for that reason, we learn to dance to their tune."

"Fidelis, thanks for walking to and from the hospital with me, I really appreciate it. You're a smart lady."

I lock the door behind her, and I feel the muscles in my throat tighten. It's like I've got a football stuck there. I put my hands to my aching throat and pace from the small living/dining area where two air-conditioners rattle and hum to the Pullman kitchen with its compact washer and dryer, small stove, and un-deluxe refrigerator. Then I go to the spare room, the bedroom, the bathroom, and start over again. It's like I am looking for something, but I know that I'm not. The ache in my throat is more intense now. I throw myself on the lumpy bed that smells like a hamper stuffed with dirty socks. I shed tears until I'm dehydrated.

. . .

The doorbell rings. Damn it. I completely blocked it out. "Hi, come in, I'll be just a minute."

"Take your time," Jan says.

"No. Don't take your time. We gotta get into the Pizza Palace, place our orders and get served before the call to Prayer. That's when the world shuts down. So you better bloody hurry."

"Okay, okay, I'm ready, let's go."

"Hurry, or they'll run us down," Jan says as she tugs my elbow while crossing the street.

"They drive like bloody maniacs," Carolyn chimes in. "Car accidents are a big problem here. They keep the ER busy. It's dangerous just to cross a road here."

"But there are so few cars on the road," I say. Why do I even bother to comment? I wish these two would stop with the stories.

"I used to ride a bicycle, but I sold it. I was afraid they'd run me down. They drive right up on the sidewalks. You'll see little boys behind the wheel sometimes, too," Carolyn says.

"Just no women," Jan says. "What did you think of the place today, Kelly?"

"Very interesting. I think I'll like the job."

A look crosses between them. It's quiet. We're the only three people on the streets as we hurry to the Pizza Palace, and we've walked about a quarter of a mile.

The Pizza Palace is a bright and clean restaurant organized like a McDonald's. The aroma of freshly baked pizza dough is comforting but at the same time makes me homesick. This place probably seats twenty. "We need to sit over there behind the partition—in the family section. Not in the open area where the men sit," Carolyn says.

"I recommend the Palace Special," says quiet Jan. "It's a New York style thin crust with everything on it—mushrooms, peppers, onion, pepperoni, and olives. A large costs forty-nine riyals. That's about thirteen dollars or four something each. I'll place the order if you want me to."

"Yeah, sure," I say and Carolyn agrees.

Jan gets up and goes to the counter.

"Don't be alarmed if you get any crank phone calls. Your predecessor got them all the time," says Carolyn out of the blue. "Better stay away from any disciplinary actions or your staff will sabotage you with more than the bloody crank calls."

Then she goes on to advise me, "You ought to listen to the bloody sermons that are preached from the mosques on Friday evenings. They broadcast it on loud speakers so you can hear it all over this bloody place. Quite chilling, really. It's delivered in Arabic, naturally. My sources tell me that the preacher admonishes the Saudis not to become like the unholy and decadent Westerners. You can hear the wrath in his bloody voice. It reminds me of Hitler."

"Fifteen years of this? You are an enigma to me, Carolyn." I just created tension and wish I hadn't. The pizza is placed on the table. The tension dissipates as we watch the proprietor of the Pizza Palace lock the front door, pull the drapes over the windows and dim the lights. No new customers to be admitted; it is evening prayer time. The proprietor disappears. We are, however, permitted to stay in the restaurant.

On the way back to Camp Five, a young Western woman whizzes by us on a bike and waves. I am told by Carolyn the woman is Inger Iverson, lady about town and ICU head nurse. Jan adds, "She's got quite a reputation."

Carolyn prattles on about Inger's lifestyle of party going with all the men in town. I try to tune her out. They really can pour on the stories and they're all so negative. If all or even some of what they say is true, it's really a scary place. We say good night at the door to 5350. I'm determined not to let their stories get to me.

I flip open a can of diet Seven-Up. The doorbell rings and I jump—my stomach does a flip-flop.

"Hi, I'm Inger Iverson. I saw a light on so I figured I'd pay you a welcome visit."

"Come in, come in."

"How nice of you. Her purple Fila warm-up suit fits her voluptuous body perfectly. She looks like a movie star. "Sit down. May I offer you something to drink—coffee … ?"

"No thanks. I didn't get to meet you today but, I've heard all about you. What you look like, what you wore today and how long you were in Mr. Al Kahairi's office."

"Tell me about yourself."

"I am here to recruit you to join the women's softball team. Having a social life, fun activities, exercise, and getting on the party list is the only way to survive, believe me. Softball season starts this Wednesday evening with tryouts. You recruit Fidelis. I've heard you're pals with her. We need a lot of players—the dropout rate is high."

We say good night and I begin to search thru my unpacked suitcase for an outfit for tomorrow. I'll clean the closet and wash out the dresser drawers before I unpack tomorrow. Maybe Carolyn and Jan are just jealous of the beautiful blonde with the great figure. I can't buy into Carolyn's version of a rule-breaking prostitute whom everyone hates. I like her. She's refreshing.

I shower, shampoo my hair, put on a gown, get into the lumpy bed and think about joining the women's softball team. I'll broach the subject with Fidelis tomorrow. I look at my diary on the bedside stand given to me by my dear deceased aunt who supported my decision to embark on this adventure. I remember her saying so sweetly and distinctly, "In the end, we regret most the things that we didn't do."

Chapter 4

Tuesday, September 15, 1987

Fidelis rings my doorbell at 7:20 a.m. Off we go into the hot sun, hot air, and hellish chore of watching out for stray cats.

I check in with Angelita. The expression on her face and the tone of her voice suggests amusement as she tells me that I am due in the conference room for my first team meeting.

Seated at the head of an oval shaped blonde wooden table, is Mr. Al Kahairi. On his right sits Dr. Small and on his left is someone I've not met before. He stands, extends his hand, and grins.

"Kelly, I'm Richard Savage from Engineering and IS—welcome to our little team." He looks like so many young white American males you see in television soap operas.

"Nice to meet you. Good morning, Mr. Al Kahairi, Dr. Small." I slip into the chair next to Richard that is covered in a beige fabric that looks and feels like a worn out Turkish towel. There's a dead silence. I look around the room and note the walls are painted a lifeless eggshell. The absence of decorations is striking.

Then with a smile plastered all over his boyish face, Richard says, "Mr. Al Kahairi was just telling us a shocking story—well, you tell it," he nods to Al Kahairi.

Mr. Al Kahairi tells the story. Apparently somebody informed the Authority that Moktar is blackmailing a female patient. They say Moktar often eavesdrops while covering switchboard and that is how he learned of this woman's love affair with her cousin. She's Laila Albalawi, a Saudi, mother of five, in room 110 for a broken leg, married to a much older man. Supposedly Moktar is threatening to tell her husband if she doesn't agree to a liaison with him.

"If Moktar is found guilty ..." Mr. Al Kahairi raises his right hand, presses it hard against his fat neck and moves it slowly from left to right.

As though on cue, Richard rises from his chair and in a stage whisper says, "And for the adulterous whore who brings disgrace to her family," mimicking a Cy Young Award winner, winds up and throws and says, "death by stoning," then dramatically drops in his chair.

"What Moktar and that woman are doing is dangerous and unacceptable in this culture," says Al Kahairi.

"It's dangerous and unacceptable in any culture," I blurt out.

Mr. Al Kahairi says, "We must take action, do something to show the Authority that we're dealing with this problem. This looks bad for us. He's our employee."

Dr. Small scratches his ear and says, "This is not my area. I don't want to get involved. Miss Day, this is your area, isn't it? I mean the ER, switchboard, among other things."

"Well, I, ah, don't quite know what to make of this situation. This is my second day—I am a nurse not a ..."

Richard cuts me off. "You're a member of this administrative team now," he says.

"We have to tell the Authority that we did something while they investigate," Al Kahairi says.

The three men stare at me. I take a deep breath and let it out slowly. "I'll suspend him from working the switchboard until further notice. He can continue as driver and language interpreter and whatever else he does." My rotten luck—just after I thought we'd established a good rapport on the way back from getting my photo taken yesterday.

The team disperses, and Richard follows me into my office, and without asking, sits down. "Kelly, don't look so worried. It's no big deal. This kind of thing goes on all the time. This is my second go around in Saudi. By the way, everybody calls me Rick."

"Where are you from?"

A grin spreads across his pretty face. "Climax, Colorado."

"Never heard of it."

"You?"

"Ashtabula, Ohio."

Rick bursts into song, "I'll look for you in old Honolulu, San Francisco, Ashtabula …"

"Stop right there. I can't afford to even think of Ashtabula. I'm homesick."

"Bob Dylan, You're Gonna Make Me Lonesome When You Go, one of my favorites. I'm a big fan."

"Me too."

"I know it's a huge adjustment. I'm here to help you adjust." Again, he grins.

"You think I should lighten up. Don't you?"

"Yes, Miss Day, I do."

"Rick, I know Moktar has got to be innocent."

He bursts into laughter, holds his sides, and gets up from the chair. He takes steps towards the door, turns back towards me, and with emphasis on each word says, "Never, never, never, never trust a Saudi." He disappears.

My first administrative team meeting and we're dealing with the potential of Moktar getting his head chopped off and some young woman getting stoned to death. It doesn't get any better than this.

I call Steve and ask him to come to my office. He's in my office in a flash and asks, "How did your meeting go with the King, the Dick, and the Doctor?"

"Honestly, Steve. Let's get serious here." I tell him I need to meet with Moktar, and I'll be informing him that he is not to relieve the switchboard operators until further notice. I tell Steve to rearrange Moktar's schedule and make sure he gets all his hours. Steve believes that King Khaled is out to get Moktar and that he's a fool to tangle with him. Steve goes on to tell me that when he first arrived here, five young Filipino chaps in his department were being deported because they were alleged to be homosexuals. Moktar went to Mr. Al Kahairi and tried to save one of the chaps from losing his job and getting deported. No luck. Then he wrote to King Fahd. Allegedly, Moktar was credited for saving the chap's job.

"Moktar knows everybody; he has a lot of friends. I'd never cross him. Actually, he's a good fellow. I'll bet this is about Lady Laila with the broken leg—she's awfully amusing."

"Steve, my focus is on relieving Moktar of his switchboard duty. Bring him by this afternoon—say about three?"

"No problem." He shakes his head and mumbles, "Rubbish."

I sign a handful of overtime slips, approve employee work schedules for next month and perform a few other routine tasks. I watch the clock because I need to avoid prayer time so that the restaurant and shops will be open when I take my lunch break.

Exiting through a door on the east wing of the hospital, I walk about one hundred yards in the blistering sun to a plaza. A water fountain jets about five feet into the air and splashes down into a pond providing a centerpiece for the plaza and the only sound and movement in the area. Clusters of green shrubs are wrapped in low stone walls, which are topped with slabs of marble where folks may rest but no one is seated there now. Evenly spaced palm trees, modern lamp posts, and concrete canopies over sidewalks add to the beauty and dramatic simplicity of the area. The plaza is flanked on the north, west and south by neat strips of small shops and businesses. To the east is a large contemporary white mosque with its minaret towering above the plaza like the steeple of a church over a small town. It makes me think of Ashtabula, with its many churches.

Although the setting is lovely, the shops are disappointingly dull. Men staff the shops, run the businesses, and only a few men are shopping. Some men stare at me while others look past me.

I am delighted to see a newspaper and magazine rack on the sidewalk in front of an office supply store. Newspapers in languages that I don't recognize pass before my eyes as I turn the rack. Happiness is stumbling upon a USA Today. I part with nine riyals, which is the equivalent of two dollars and forty cents.

On devilish Steve's recommendation, I enter the Big Bun sandwich shop which is very clean, new looking, and the smallest snack shop I've ever been in. I study the laminated menu posted on an otherwise bare wall. The limited selection of lamb or chicken, with or without vegetables, come on a toasted bun. I love the distinctive smell of lamb cooking. It makes me think about the Greek restaurant back home in my neighborhood.

"I like the lamb. You should try it," says a dark-skinned man in Western clothes with an accent from I don't know where.

I smile. I place my order with the clerk and sit at the only available small table. The only way to separate the sexes here is to sit at different tables. I glance at the headlines and the stranger asks, "Anything interesting?"

I look up and say, "Not really."

The clerk delivers my lamb with vegetables on a very big toasted bun on a paper plate and a diet Pepsi in a paper cup.

The stranger who's sitting so close to me he could eat off my plate, asks, "May I join you?"

"No, I believe it is against the law."

He tries again. "You're new here, aren't you?"

I look at him, shake my head. Does the USA Today signal decadent Western whore?

He stands, pays his bill, places a folded note on my table, and leaves. I open the note: There is no law prohibiting talking on the phone. ZAYNAB 4020244. His printing has a unique slant to it—very neat as well.

I immediately tear the note up for the benefit of the clerk in the event that he'd been watching. Possibly he could report this suspicious behavior. And, I have no interest in this stranger.

I approach the clerk to pay my bill and he informs me that "the guy paid it." I want to say to the clerk, "You did see me destroy the note didn't you?" But I keep my mouth shut.

.   .   .

I return to the hospital and as I walk down the corridor to my office, a friendly voice calls out to me, "You're Kelly Day, aren't you?"

"Yes, I am and, who are you?"

"I'm Beverly Ann Bruce. All the ex-pats, well really mostly the male ex-pats," she chuckles, "are talking about the pretty young thing who just arrived in town and who is afraid of cats. I thought I'd mosey by and see for myself," says this robust woman with a Texas accent.

"Really, I'm here to encourage you to join the women's softball league. It's great fun," she exclaims with the exuberance of a cheer-leader for the Dallas Cowboys. "The best part is that it's two evenings out a week. Two big evenings at the Saudi Turf."

Her enthusiasm seems forced. "Would you like to sit in my office and chat for a while?"

"Yeah, I've got time."

We sit at the round table in front of the picture window.

"Nice office. I wish I had a job." She's large, plump, and looks very sad.

"How is it that you're living here?"

"I'm here with my husband. Bob, my husband, lost his job in the oil industry back home in Houston. This opportunity seemed like a quick fix to a rapidly mounting debt. So it's his fault we're stuck in this damn sand trap. But I'm going to get unstuck—I'm going to leave him. Sure, he's needed here for his expertise as an executive in the oil business. He's lucky. He enjoys his work. But I'm bored to death and not needed for anything. I hate it here."

"I'm really sorry."

"Oh, don't worry about me. I'm going home for Christmas and I'm not coming back." She takes a deep breath and exhales like she's relieved of a big burden.

I feel sorry for her. I wonder if she'll regret it later that she shared so much personal stuff.

She grunts and stands up. I get up also. Bev puts her arm around my shoulder as I walk her to the main lobby. She says that the uniform for the tryouts at the Saudi Turf is a long sleeved shirt, preferably one that covers your ass, and baggy slacks.

We say goodbye, and then over her shoulder she shouts, "If you come to the tryouts—and I hope you do—you'll meet the son-of-a-bitch who dragged me here. He's one of the coaches."

I wince, as I am confident that shouting "son-of-a-bitch" is against the law.

Angelita who again appears amused by what I don't know, stops by my office to tell me Mr. Al Kahairi wants to see me in his office now.

"Thank you, Angelita. Know what it's about?"

"Nope."

Off she goes. Why do I think she does know?

On my way to Mr. al Kahairi's offiice I'm approached by Violeta, a vivacious nurse whom I met when Steve toured me around.

She's direct and assertive. "Please come to my place tonight at 6:00 p.m. I'm hosting a birthday party for one of your nurses—Michelle Martinez—you won't see her very often, she works exclusively nights in the newborn nursery. My place—5480."

"Wonderful, I'll be there." Her enthusiasm is so contagious, I would have responded positively to a knitting party. Of course, I don't know how I'm going to get there on my own. But, I'll have a place to go—something to do—it'll fill an evening and I'll get to know more hospital workers. There'll be food—I won't have to cook.

Oh boy, is the birthday party one of those unusual events or gatherings that I'm supposed to inform him about? Well, I won't share this because I think it is silly, and I don't want to set a precedent. I wonder what he wants now.

"I have something for you." He smiles, and hands me an envelope.

"What a pleasant surprise. This is my very first piece of mail, thanks."

"How are you finding things … the staff—helpful?"

"Yes, everything is fine."

"If you need anything, anything at all, please let me know."

"Thank you." Do I need anything? What's he doing with my mail? This is the first time in my life that I feel as though I can't trust anyone. No doubt there are trustworthy people here, but I just haven't encountered them yet, except of course for Fidelis.

I retreat to my office, shut the door, and savor every word of my mother's humorous letter that she wrote and mailed before I left Ashtabula to be sure I got mail my first week in Yanbu. I am the product of two very doting and supportive parents. The downside is that it has taken me a little longer to grow up or maybe even wise up.

My phone rings, and I'll bet it's Jan. She called me twice yesterday to ask, "How are things going?"

"Hello, Jan."

"How are things going?"

"Fine."

"Are you going to Michelle's birthday party?"

"Yes, as a matter of fact, I am."

"I'm going too. Let me stop by and get you. You'll never find her place the way the units are numbered."

I ask her about the mail, and I learn that Moktar picks it up at the post office every afternoon except Fridays. He brings it to Mr. Al Kahairi's office, from there it goes to Angelita who sorts it and puts it out on the table in the hallway by three in the afternoon. You may not receive all your mail because at the post office it's censored on a random basis and confiscated at their discretion. The same with packages—anything political or religious other than Islamic is considered contraband. Sometimes you may not get letters for no apparent reason. They're just missing. Some ex-pats don't put their return address on their outgoing mail because if the censors are offended, they don't want it traced back to them. I'm cautioned not to complain to my family and friends about the customs. I remember some of those folks I interviewed by phone prior to coming here telling me I might not get all my mail. But I assumed the failure was due to a systems problem and not for reason of intolerance.

I reread my letter, laugh out loud, and cry. I examine the postage stamps on the envelope. The red, white and blue waves across the top half of these bright little squares. The lower half is a sketch of the Capitol building. USA is in bold type and the number 22 under it indicating the cost of the stamp. What a beautiful sight. I carefully cut one of the stamps from the envelope and lean it against the base of my desk lamp.

The dreaded meeting is upon me. Steve, Moktar, and I exchange pleasantries while sitting around the small table in my office.

Steve says, "What do you get from a pampered goat?"

"Tell us," Moktar says.

"Spoiled milk."

Moktar laughs. I fake a laugh. I'm wondering how Moktar will react to no more switchboard. Does he really have all those big connections?

I tell Moktar that I'd like him to focus more on his role as interpreter and on assisting those patients who need help filling out paper work and discontinue switchboard duty for now. He raises his eyebrows and stares into my eyes. I hold my breath. The silence is deafening. At last he speaks.

"No problem."

End of workday. I'm leaving a little early. After all, I've a party to go to tonight.

Steve catches me on the way to Fidelis' office and says, "I talked with Moktar before our meeting and smoothed the way for you."

I give him a fake smile and keep going. Something's bugging me about him.

Next, I hear Dr. Small call out to me. He waves me into his office. He tells me to sit down, and that what he has to say won't take long.

He says, "I think, can't prove it, and don't know for sure but Khaled supposedly hates Moktar. I don't know why, really. I'm not sure the story about Moktar blackmailing the patient is true." He says just above a whisper, "Moktar has contacts at the Authority—a relative, I think. Apparently, he knows everybody, they say." He scratches his ear—flakes of skin fall on his lapel.

Just my luck. Moktar will turn out to be the favorite nephew of the Custodian of the two Holy Mosques, King Fahd of the Kingdom of Saudi Arabia and I just told him that he can't work the switchboard.

On the way to 5350 I ask Fidelis to join the softball team—or at least go to the tryouts tomorrow. She's fine with it.

.   .   .

"This will be different, you'll see," Jan says on our brief walk to the birthday party.

She's starting to annoy me, but I'm glad she and Carolyn bought the severe life-threatening allergy story about the cats because it helps to have a companion who is willing to shoo cats away.

We enter the party and I'm jolted by the sight of a group of women dancing with each other. Petite women gyrating to a disco beat who look more like teenagers than women in their early twenties. They're a feminine and chic bunch, clad in colorful sundresses, halter tops, designer jeans, and matching skirts and blouses. Make-up carefully applied, perfumed and jeweled, they sport trendy haircuts. They look bright and fresh, like a bouquet of spring flowers.

I get a lump in my throat knowing that many of these women have husbands, a baby or two, parents, and grandparents back in the Phillipines. Bread-winners for their large families more than five thousand miles away. I can't imagine what it's like for these young women to come all this way, work so hard in a foreign culture, and send the money home. It must take a ton of fortitude to endure the separation of family let alone the adjustment to a culture with more rules than one can keep up with.

About twenty-five women are packed into the standard Camp Five two-bedroom unit. Over-sized red, orange and yellow flowers made of tissue paper are fixed to the walls with tape as well as other handmade decorations and a zillion family photos.

The place is hot in spite of three air-conditioners turned on high. The noise level is turned on high, too. Superficial bits of conversation shouted over the blasting Sony cassette player in English and Tagalog with a little Arabic thrown in adds levity to an already spirited group.

Violeta is wearing a red sun-dress, gobs of make-up and jewelry galore. She leads me to an inviting buffet table. The odors are divine—the garlic seductive. She explains many of the girls, as she calls them, brought specially prepared dishes for which they're known.

"There's Cora's barbequed chicken wings; Maritza's three rice dishes; Nielda's lush green salad; Maria's sculpted fruit in jello con-conction; and a wonderful dish called pancit, prepared by Gilda."

I'm introduced to Gilda. She explains, "Pancit is made up of tiny pieces of chicken, finely chopped vegetables sautéed in garlic and oil, noodles, and must be served warm."

Soft drinks, coffee, and tea are offered. A fancy decorated sheet cake bears the message: Happy Birthday, Michelle, We Love You. I calm my labile emotions with the satisfying food and eat more than my share of the pancit.

There is entertainment, too. Using a home-party player with a microphone, sensuous Violeta belts out one love ballad after another. She is rewarded with cheers and applause. Next she gives a tribute and dedicates a song to the honored birthday celebrant.

Fancy crafted greeting cards and gifts are presented to Michelle.

Michelle thanks her friends in an emotional and touching speech. Dozens of photos are snapped. The lump in my throat is back. Others pull out their hankies and openly shed tears as they applaud her sweet testimonial to friendship and love. I'm moved by the strong sense of community.

Violeta calls for everyone to dance and eat some more. The music is turned up and the swift dance movements again dominate the room to Lionel Richie's, Dancing on the Ceiling. It is clear to me that beneath the gaiety, the struggle to deal with the wrenching loneliness persists.

I'm back at 5350 by ten, sitting alone in my dungeon. I've had a full day with a parade of new people. I wish I had someone I could talk to about all that's happened. I'm going to write in my diary. I feel too tense to even think about trying to sleep.

In my entire life I've never been through anything like this. I hope I don't go bananas here. According to the textbooks, culture shock is anxiety due to an abrupt loss of familiar signs and symbols of a well-known and well-understood environment. I won't despair. I'm normal. I'll make it. I'm confident I can get through another day. The young women at the party tonight are making it work.

Chapter 5

Wednesday, September 16, 1987.

It's 7:20 a.m. Fidelis rings my doorbell on this morning that is just like yesterday morning—too hot, an absence of fluffy white clouds, too quiet, no birds chirping, but cats crawling around like they own the town. Fidelis looks pensive and is quiet this morning. I decide to inquire about Moktar.

She hesitates. "You've asked me about Moktar before, Kelly. I rarely have contact with him."

I stop walking, look her straight in the eyes. "Fidelis, that's not an answer."

We resume walking. "Be careful with him, Kelly. Now this is just gossip, and you know how I hate gossip. It can do so much harm."

"For God's sake, say it, Fidelis."

"I once overheard a clerk at the office supply store in the mall refer to Moktar as a 'one man mafia.' Kelly, you just arrived here. Look and listen, tuck things away, suspend judgment."

"Thank you, Fidelis. I'll try."

Upon my arrival at the hospital, six nurses squeeze into my office. They're all talking at once about a wall that's going to be built around Camp Five.

"I'll break my contract if that happens," says Inger.

"Me too," says Poey a Muslim nurse from Thailand. "When I worked in the Eastern Province, our living quarters were surrounded by a wall and all of us women were required to sign in and sign out each and every time we left our Camp. We resented it."

Complaining continues followed by more firm promises to break contracts if a wall goes up around Camp Five.

"I hear your frustration. The threat of a wall with all the control it symbolizes is irksome. It seems punitive, I agree. I'll bring this up at the administrative meeting."

The women leave wearing long faces.

I tell the administrative team about the meeting with the nurses. Dr. Small looks perplexed and says, "This is the first I've heard of it." He turns to Mr. Al Kahairi for help.

Khaled leans back in his chair as if to distance himself from us or the subject (maybe both). "If they don't see a wall, they shouldn't worry."

Rick Savage doodles on a yellow legal pad. I bite a finger nail, and Dr. Small scratches his ear. The little conference room is library-quiet.

Khaled shifts in his chair, squares his shoulders and breaks the silence. "I recommend that a trip to the beach be planned for the girls."

Rick snickers and continues to doodle. I cringe and bite another fingernail.

Dr. Small belts out, "What a great idea. That's super." His forced cheerfulness bounces off the eggshell colored walls. He seems totally unaware that he is a cheerful party of one.

Then with the veracity and creative energy of a greedy millionaire searching for a tax loophole, Khaled dives into the now top priority of planning the girls' beach party. He shoots orders my way. "Miss Day, get all the girls you can to commit, keep the list locked in your desk drawer, don't circulate anything in print, keep this low-profile, and make sure at least one of the girls is a lifeguard."

Dr. Small and Rick sit quietly as the team of King Khaled and Kelly begin in earnest to plan the top priority, low-profile "Nurse's Day at the Beach." Khaled will arrange a driver for the bus, a lead car, and two-way radios in case the bus breaks down because it will travel to a remote area.

"The radio thing is a good idea, but why the lead car?" I ask my co-conspirator.

"We can't trust that the bus driver would not tell the location to the girls' boyfriends and they'd show up at the beach. The Saudi in the lead car will also act as hospital representative if the police stop the bus."

I'll do my best to facilitate the beach party—it strikes me as both funny and sad.

Rick follows me to my office and drifts into a litany of complaints mixed with wisecracks and jokes centering on the lack of good alcohol, the prohibition of mingling of the sexes, the dearth of social events, and the meager entertainment industry that consists of three channels on government-controlled television.

"Sure there's women's softball to coach, but no cold beers in a sports bar afterwards. I just want to get laid every night. Stock-piling cash isn't all that it's cracked up to be."

.   .   .

"We've got a drunk princess and a lacerated scrotum!" Steve shouts to me as I enter the ER.

"For heaven's sake, Steve, not so loud. Fill me in on the princess first, then the guy."

"The little princess was so drunk we had to get three nurses to help her from the car to a wheelchair. Then, to get the princess from the wheelchair to the cart in cubicle eight, we had to call around to all the departments to find one more female. Try that at 5:30 a.m. when the night nurses are busy finishing their paperwork and preparing for the change of shift."

"So, you're telling me that if a female patient has three female nurses in attendance and another pair of hands is needed for lifting, a male may not assist."

"Precisely. Now don't you want to know just how drunk the princess was?"

"Okay, just how drunk was the princess?"

"Blood alcohol 465. We'll monitor for withdrawal and treat as indicated."

"Wow." I take a peak in cubicle eight. The princess must weigh all of three hundred pounds. Her mouth is wide open, spittle in the corners, and she is snoring like an old man.

"Steve, are you pulling my leg? She can't be a real princess. All princesses have tiny waistlines, delicate hands, small feet, and they definitely don't snore. Of course, I've never met one, but I've read about them and have seen enough pictures in story books."

"Now, do you want to see the lacerated scrotum?"

"Stop it, Steve. Is he going to be all right?"

"It's touch and go. He's bleeding—the laceration is 25 centimeters long."

"You're exaggerating, but go on."

"We can't get him to surgery until the alcohol is out of his system. Besides, he's so drunk he's not competent to sign a consent for surgery. He was the driver of the car. Empty bottles of liquor were found in the car. Lucky for him he didn't hit someone or something. Unlucky in another way, however."

"How did the laceration occur? Never mind forget I asked. What's going to happen to them?"

"The little princess won't have a problem. She is a princess, after all. The poor bloke will have a lot of explaining to do. Jail time for sure. Every cut, no matter how minor, requires, a police report. So, my lady, if you cut your finger while preparing dinner tonight and came here to have it sewn up, a police report would be mandatory."

"But, if the princess cut his ..."

Steve's eyes twinkle, "The dumbest bloke on this planet earth would know better than to accuse a princess of a crime. By Jove, that would be his death sentence."

"I gotta go."

"I'll call you when the little princess wakes up. She speaks fine English in spite of her uncivilized behavior. You can have a little chat with her, but it won't be as much fun if she's sobered up by then."

"Don't call me."

. . .

I'm on my way back to my office when I'm ambushed by Bev Bruce from Texas. She says, "I just came from my physical therapy appointment with the bold and the restless physical therapist, Mahmoud. He's treating my sprained thumb." She waves her hand in my face and grins like a school girl. "Let's have lunch at the Big Bun—if that's okay with you? That's where I first met Mahmoud just a week ago."

"Your timing is perfect, Bev. I'm ready for lunch."

We approach the counter, and Bev calls the clerk, Hakim, and tells him she'll have her usual. I order the lamb sandwich.

Bev strikes up a conversation with the two men at the table next to us and one of them happens to be Zaynab. I nod at him politely. They are Egyptians who work at the desalination plant. They want to know all about us. Where are we from, do we work, and where, doing what. Bev answers for both of us and then invites them to the Saudi Turf to watch the women's softball games.

I ask her if she's aware of how potentially dangerous mingling can be. She laughs and says the Big Bun is the speakeasy for those who desire to mingle. Lord, have mercy on me. I hit the speakeasy twice within my first five days in the Kingdom. She ends our conversation abruptly because she sees someone she knows and she wants to catch up with him.

. . .

Inger, Fidelis, and I reach the Saudi Turf as the big blue sky begins to fade to a grayish white. Two baseball diamonds, electric lights, field house and bleacher seats look like Anywhere, USA, except for the lack of green grass. I'd give anything to smell freshly cut grass right now.

Inger quips, "Here come the girls in their white stretch limo." The white rickety hospital shuttle bus unloads about a dozen Filipino nurses.

"Welcome softball chicks," says Rick Savage as he swaggers towards us. "The turn out is good—we've got the little nurses from the hospital and the mal-contented housewives from the Married Couples Camp."

"Really, Rick." I throw him a look.

Then we hear Bob shout over the crowd's noisy and happy chatter for us to listen up. He introduces himself and the seven other men who will serve as coaches, umpires, and score-keepers. We are instructed to count off—one, two, three, four. In my opinion there is nothing about Bob that conjures up notions of a "son-of-a-bitch."

Each of the four groups gets a coach assigned to them. Lucky for the "ones," we get that tall, muscular, trim guy with broad shoulders, coal black hair and a knock-out smile. Dan Gutierrez from Dallas. He should be a model for designer t-shirts and jeans.

First, Dan assesses each one's knowledge of the rules of the game. I have no knowledge. Second, he asks about our experience. I have no experience. The ultimate humiliation comes when we get to demonstrate our skills. I have no skills. Can't throw the ball. Can't catch the ball. Can't hit the ball. A few women, including Fidelis, demonstrate some skill, and several women look like pros. Dan is writing notes in a little book.

With the sincerity and vigor of an unjaded junior high school coach, Dan says, "In the past, I've watched many rookies develop skills in just a matter of weeks—with practice, that is—become good players by the end of the season." He flashes a smile. "We're going to have fun."

Bob calls us together again. He tells us that we'll get our team assignment when we return on Saturday. A plea is made not to drop out because they desperately want to maintain four teams and that's just about what we have tonight. He further cautions us to, "Be discreet. Two of the seven men are single and if 'they' find out, the games could be discontinued." He pleads, "Ladies and gentlemen, no socializing. Take the game seriously, work hard, and we'll all have a good season. Good night now."

Our little hospital gang gathers together, except for Inger who's with Rick and the guys. There is much joking about the tryouts and how we all qualified regardless of our skill level and talk about handsome Dan, dirty Dick, and what a great guy Bob seems to be.

Violeta, the singer and hostess from last night's party launches into a little speech that she calls, "Words of Caution." She clears her throat and begins, "Remember, no laughing, no loud talking, no socializing with the coaches, umpires, or male spectators. Male spectators can only be the husbands of the women players—no boyfriends allowed—wear modest clothing and very little face paint. She laughs and tosses her catcher's mitt high into the air and yells, "Forget about the wall—play ball!"

Dan approaches me and Violeta teases with a shake of her finger, "You could be looking at jail time, Miss Day." There's more loud laughter.

Before I can say anything, Dan pulls me off to the side and says, "I'm glad you came here tonight. I enjoy teaching the game and working with people who are new to the sport. So, welcome."

"Gee, that's nice of you but ..."

He interrupts, "We've got to get you the right bat. So, let's try this one."

"Okay."

"Place this at your side—let your arms hang loose—too short." He replaces it with another. "Just a little too long. Try this one ... nope."

"Maybe I'm not meant to play this game."

"You're not getting off that easy."

"Try this one—it's a Louisville Slugger. Give it a swing—how does it feel?"

"Not so heavy on my wrist."

"Great. Take it home with you. Practice in front of a mirror. The more comfortable you feel with your weapon the more confidence you'll take to each at bat—stepping up to the plate will be fun, not dreadful." He winks.

Dear Lord—Zaynab should take lessons from him.

Inger, Fidelis and I start our walk home. I've got my bat under my arm. The rest of our hospital gang elect to wait for the white stretch limo.

Inger tells us that she and Rick are an "item." I ask her about being afraid of getting caught. She says, "I need the relationship to survive—I'm neither a martyr nor a saint."

Inger points out the women and children's pool where I can go tomorrow afternoon as I, like the rest of the management team, get Thursday afternoons off and all day Friday. I invite my friends to come in for coffee or a cold beverage. Inger declines as she is expecting a call from Rick.

"Let's sit at the table. I hate to have my guests sit on that ugly couch with the cigarette burns."

Fidelis teases, "You're a spoiled American."

I feel my face get red. "I suppose I am. Seven-Up okay with you?"

"Sure—no ice. I'll drink it from the can."

I put a bowl of peanuts along with the cold cans of Seven-Up on the table. I flip the cap on the top of the can and enjoy the sounds of the crack and hiss.

"Do you drink beer?"

"Yeah, when I'm in the Phillipines—San Miguel—the best."

We both laugh and raise our cans and click them together.

"So tell this spoiled brat from a small town in Ohio what's a nice, smart woman from the Phillipines doing in this small town along the Red Sea, the very one that Moses parted."

"Life for me was going good until the hotel I worked for had a major fire. It was a large four-star hotel in the downtown area of Manila. I had a big job—executive director of housekeeping. I enjoyed it so much. Vendors entertained me and I entertained them. I had the authority to take them to lunch in any one of our five restaurants. And, they would take me for dinner to the restaurant of my choosing, anywhere in Manila."

She takes a sip from the can, shakes her head. "You never want to be a part of or ever witness people pushing, shoving, coughing, screaming, and crying, fleeing from smoke, flames, and falling debris. I can't turn on a gas stove or watch someone light a cigarette. I will never again enter a large hotel as long as I live."

"How horrible. I can't imagine."

"The hotel was never rebuilt. Those of us who survived couldn't find work. I'm the provider for my mother, my father and his widowed sister. Unemployment is high and wages are low back home. So here I am—seven years later."

"I am really sorry, Fidelis."

"So now it's your turn."

"I lost my job as a nursing supervisor at a hospital back in Ashtabula due to downsizing—that's what we call layoffs. I welcomed the layoff as an excuse to leave Ashtabula. The week before the layoff, I discovered that my so-called best friend and my boyfriend were having an intimate relationship. I, of course, was the last to know. I felt like a fool. Hurt and humiliated, all I wanted to do was run away and hide. So here I am a mere seven weeks later."

We sit in silence.

"That's too bad, Kelly. Deception can really hurt."

"Well, I'm okay. Let's talk about softball."

"I've played on teams before and it can be fun. That's a good bat Dan gave you."

I blush, "I guess so."

"I should go. I don't know about you but, I am very tired. The tryouts wore me out."

"Actually, I'm a little wired. I'm going to do a load or two of laundry. Anyway, I'm glad we're playing ball and hopefully we'll be on the same team."

"Teammates would be good."

We say good night.

I put the peanuts back in the jar and throw the soda cans in a trash bag. I tear open a giant box of TIDE. I love the look of the big, strong, confident, and neat container. The navy blue letters of TIDE spelled out against the excitement, dynamism and drama of a pure orange background—the sturdy box boasts an attitude of can-do optimism coupled with an independent spirit. I load the washer and add the soap powder—the irrepressible scent of the soap powder is good and clean. It was my good fortune to have been raised in the United States of America.

I know Fidelis was teasing me about being a spoiled American but it struck a chord with me. I'm a little naïve, or maybe even a lot naïve, but spoiled is not how I ever would have described myself until now. The fire that Fidelis experienced and the financial responsibility for family that she carries are mind-boggling. I'm a young woman with two retired parents who have money in the bank. I have a good education, and good health. I really didn't need to come here. A break-up and a layoff are not catastrophes especially within the context of my entire circumstances.

Laundry folded and stacked. Shower taken. I need a good night's sleep. I pull the chain on the bedside lamp and think about Fidelis, the fire, the wall, the beach party, Bev's unhappy situation and her careless behavior as well as Inger's that makes me so uneasy, the fat princess—apparently she has problems too, and my elderly parents.

On one hand, I want to run all the way back to Ashtabula, sleep in my own bed and have coffee in the kitchen with my parents in the morning. On the other hand, I want to stay here and have Dan coach me to become a competent softball player or something like that.

Chapter 6

Thursday, September 17, 1987

"Are you okay? You don't look rested," I ask Fidelis.

"The tryouts really wore me out. The heat doesn't usually bother me—but it does this morning. I'll be alright. Kelly, why are you carrying that bat?"

"Please don't laugh but—since you are going to work all day and I'm free to leave at noon—I thought I could use the bat to shoo cats away or I could just tap it on the sidewalk—I think it should work."

"Creative, I'll say. But some day—promise me, you'll see a psychiatrist about it."

We laugh.

"Feel better, my friend."

I try to hide the bat in folds of my long-full skirt as I walk quickly down the corridor to my office. Inger's waiting outside my office door.

"Don't ask."

"No, I won't. I'm here on more important business. Rick is housesitting for a bigwig at Aramco—the bigwig and his wife are off to Bali for a swinging R&R. So, he's throwing a party tonight for singles. I'm in charge of recruiting attractive girls—and you're on the list."

"I'm very flattered but leery. Aren't you ever ... worried?"

Inger interrupts me, "It's safe. The guys are preparing a feast for us. Dan is going to be there. Just in case you're interested. And, oh, it's a six-bedroom home with king-sized beds."

"I need to think about it—check with me later." Holy Lord, she's a daredevil and I'm a little chicken.

The administrative team meets. Khaled is out of character this morning. He's dressed Western style: white open-collared shirt, belted cream colored tailored slacks. He seems eager for the meeting to end, skillfully manipulating all parties to postpone matters until we meet again on Saturday.

He smiles, "I'm rushing to get to the airport—I'll be in Cairo for the weekend. Have fun," he bids us in a cheery voice that exudes an overtone of mockery. I watch his obese figure lumber down the hallway.

I think to myself—"have fun yourself, King Khaled conundrum." It was Carolyn who told me he has two wives—one here and one in Cairo. Damn it—he's going to have a fun weekend, and I'm stuck here with absolutely nothing to do but worry. I'll never forgive myself for getting on that first plane.

Rick follows me to my office and plops himself down in a chair. "Please come to the party tonight. We're short on women. I promised Dan I'd talk you into coming."

"Oh Rick, I just don't know. I don't want to get into trouble."

He laughs half-heartedly and says, "It's really Thursday, but tonight is my Friday night, and Friday is my Saturday day off, and it's not 1987 but 1408—lunar calendar. And this place is making a lunatic out of me. I need to get laid. Just think about it, Kelly."

He leaves. He's miserable, and guys have it easier here. I'm depressed.

.   .   .

With the Louisville Slugger tucked under my arm I walk in the hot noon sun, my wet blouse clings with perspiration, and my sunglasses slide on my nose. My purse seems heavier than usual. The streets are empty. Rarely, a car passes. The deadly heat is balanced by a deadly quiet. I pass the telephone center, a small non-descript one-story building with no landscaping wrapped around it. It's no time to call the States. There is no place to go but to 5350. I feel so alone, depressed, and like a lunatic for carrying this bat around with me.

About fifteen feet from the entrance to my small courtyard I stand paralyzed. Why didn't I conquer this phobia years ago? I tap the bat on the sidewalk three times, take a few steps, tap again louder, take a few more steps and with my arm stretched tight and bat straight out at shoulder level, I poke the bat against the wooden courtyard gate. Three scrawny cats scamper out from under the gate and scare me to death. My hands trembling, I unlatch the gate, dash to the door of 5350, fumble with the keys, drop them, pick them up, wipe my sweaty hand on my skirt, glance over my shoulder, insert key, turn, and slam the door behind me.

I miss Fidelis. She and I pretend it's perfectly normal to be constantly on guard for cats as we walk to and from the hospital. But today she gets to work all day.

I flip all three air-conditioners on high, drop on the lumpy bed, close my eyes and sleep for about an hour. I stare at the ceiling and think. It's only 2:00. I can get to and from the women's and children's pool all on my own if I take the Louisville Slugger with me.

I take a record fast shower, pull my hair into a ponytail, throw on a baggy top, full-length skirt, and sandals, and put my swimsuit in a plastic bag. I stand at the door. I can't make the decision to leave. The cats and the long walk in the hot sun are turn offs. What if there's no shade around the pool? I could get sun poisoning or become severely dehydrated and die. Or just maybe I could make some friends—feel less lonely. Yet I dread the tedious swap of background information when strangers meet. I've been through that exercise a thousand times since my arrival.

I throw the swimsuit into the bedroom and go into the narrow kitchen, open the refrigerator door, look at the few remaining cans of Seven-Up, two sticks of butter, and a covered bowl of green beans. I slam the door. Go back to the bedroom, grab the plastic bag and the bat, grit my teeth, hold my breath, and charge out of 5350 returning to the quiet streets.

I recall from last evening, the women's and children's pool is halfway between Camp Five and the Saudi Turf. Hot, sticky, and drenched in sweat, I arrive at what I think is the right place because I hear children's voices coming from the other side of a concrete wall which I'm approaching. There's no signage that I can see. I wait and listen. The squealing and laughter sound like more than just a few little kids. I follow along a winding concrete path for about ten yards that places me front and center at the women and children's pool. I am reminded of when I walked into the women's room at the King Abdul Aziz International Airport in Jeddah. I feel that same self-consciousness as I stand and gape.

There's a small round shallow pool crowded with dark-haired little tots, both boys and girls slapping the water and squealing. They're wearing colorful t-shirts and shorts. They play without plastic balls and pool toys. There's an average sized rectangular pool with a depth of about five feet at one end. It looks like so many swimming pools found in any back yard in Suburbia, USA.

The exception here is that, as expected, the swimmers and sunbathers are all female. But most noteworthy is the way the women are dressed. They're wearing headscarves—faces exposed, one-piece skirted bathing suits over long-sleeved colorful blouses and black tights. I've never seen anything like it. The majority are young mothers with little children. Some of the women are in the pool swimming, others watching the little ones, and others reclining poolside and chatting quietly.

I scan the area for cats. One brown cat appears to be sleeping—all stretched out in the only shady corner just outside what I think might be the entrance to a changing room. Again, no signage.

I want a shady corner but the best I can do is an unpadded green and yellow plastic recliner near the shallow end of the pool. I sit upright—not reclining—fully clothed with the Louisville Slugger next to me, and the plastic bag containing my bathing suit. I check my wristwatch—2:30 p.m. I slip off my sandals, unbutton my cuffs, roll up my sleeves, and reposition myself on the recliner so I can monitor the cat's behavior.

The sound of squealing tots and children at play is a pleasant sound. The sight of women dressed radically different from swimmers and sunbathers than I'm accustomed to is amusing and thought pro-voking.

The cat, however, is an entirely different story—threatening and intimidating despite being asleep—preventing me from changing into my swimsuit. I just can't go into the pool all dressed up like this. Oh well, I rationalize—wearing only a bathing suit might appear disre-spectful to the other women.

It's 3:10 p.m. I'm hungry, I'm hot, I'm tired and I'm tense from being hyper-vigilant about the brown cat. Back on my feet, I trudge to 5350 and repeat my new bat routine.

It's just me, a Seven-Up, a can of tuna fish, and it's only 3:35 p.m. I've hit the misery jackpot—too many externally imposed restrictions on behavior, and my super neurotic fear of cats in a town overrun with them. Can't speak Arabic and couldn't talk with the ladies at the pool.

I feel so cut off—it's like I'm in solitary confinement. I should go to the commissary and walk up and down the aisles. Buy stuff whether I need it or not. Stave off stir craziness.

The phone rings. I'm so glad, don't care who's at the other end of the line.

"I've been calling you."

"Well, Dan, I was out at the women's and children's pool."

"Good for you. Did you have a good swim?"

"No."

"What?"

"It's a long story."

"I'm calling to encourage you to come to Rick's party tonight. Inger told me that you're reluctant. I usually go to parties. It helps to have some social life—just chatting with Westerners and listening to their stories passes the time."

"I know you're right, but …"

"I'll call Inger and tell her to swing by around 5:30 p.m. She knows her way around all the camps."

"Okay, thanks, Dan."

. . .

I check my watch. Inger should be here any minute. I like the way I've done my hair and make-up. My matching ice blue skirt and blouse is my favorite outfit and I love my pearl necklace. But, I don't feel good—my stomach is queasy.

Inger arrives. "Come in please." She's quite glam in a red sundress. "You look great, Inger."

"Thanks, so do you."

I know she means well but I doubt she really likes my plain outfit. I look like a grade school teacher next to her.

"I can't go, Inger. I'm too chicken!"

She shakes her head. "Don't miss a fun evening, Kelly. I do this all the time. Sometimes two and three times a week. You'll be sorry and the guys will be disappointed. If you don't go, you'll probably never be invited to another party again. Trust me on this."

"Inger, I really want to go. I'm dying for a good time."

"Then for heaven's sake, just come on!"

I'm at the door, purse in hand. "No, Inger—I'm just too chicken."

"You'll be sorry."

. . .

The quiet in dungeon number 5350 is pierced again by a ringing phone. A dungeon with a phone—that's funny. I jump up and dash to answer it. Carolyn invites me to join her and Jan on a trip to Yanbu's old town tonight. I readily accept.

I change my clothes to super casual and kill a few minutes practicing my swing in front of the long mirror in the bedroom. I daydream about Dan close behind me guiding my arms through the motion of a perfect swing. Why didn't I learn to play softball in high school? So many things I didn't learn.

Carolyn and Jan ring the doorbell at 6:50 p.m. I'm told that the hospital provides transportation to and from old Yanbu every Thursday evening for the nurses of Camp Five.

The white stretch limo pulls away at 7:10 p.m. with about twenty Camp Fivers who are laughing, joking, and chatting in English and Tagalog with Arabic phrases thrown in.

The narrow aisle of the half-empty white stretch limo is flanked on both sides by about a dozen rows of dark grey pairs of joined seats. We speed along a paved road. Here and there a few cars and an occasional four-by-four passes by. Small gas stations show up as well. Then on to a dirt road for another fifteen minutes; less scenery, more sky, a few bumps in the road, my spine is jarred. The driver has maintained the same high rate of speed from the paved road to the dirt road.

At last the limo unloads a jostled but cheerful gang of young nurses at a parking area where men of all ages are loitering in twos and threes, leaning against desert-worn cars and pickup trucks. Carolyn says that they are waiting to see the nurses and later some nurses will pair off with the men in the back seats of cars.

The ratio of men to women must be at least 20 to 1. For the most part, they are men of color, some are bearded, some are clean-shaven and dressed in Western style shirts and trousers. Some are hatless, while others are wearing turbans, baseball caps and the familiar red-checkered Saudi headdress is common. More than half of them are smoking cigarettes. The thick smoke is irritating to my eyes and throat. I feel uncomfortable and intimidated being looked over by all these men as we parade past them.

The old town of Yanbu is like nothing I've ever seen before. It's about five to six acres with an abandoned construction project, decaying buildings and lots of stray cats. I notice a few Western couples (presumably married to each other) strolling in the open-air fruit and vegetable market which is crudely organized. The pungent odor of seared meat on open pit grills permeates the stagnant air and stimulates my appetite. No lines and plenty of little stands to choose from. Each vendor offers one or two items at the most.

Carolyn, Jan, and I purchase goat meat kabobs with yogurt and mint sauce and orange drinks just before prayer time. We find a resting place on cinder blocks far from the food vendors as cats circle them. I hesitate, then slowly picking up the smallest chunk of goat meat, I dip it in the sauce and place it in my mouth. It's soft, easy to chew and tastes somewhat like lamb. It's delicious. I'm relieved. I clean my plate.

We wait for the shops to re-open and vendors to return to their outdoor posts. Carolyn's noticeably quiet and surprisingly a little sad as she comments, "everything I'm doing here tonight is for the last time."

Bev comes charging towards me out of nowhere and insists that I join her and Bob. I tell Carolyn and Jan I will catch up with them later.

Bev asks, "What are you doing tomorrow?"

I shake my head. "Really, I have no idea."

"Well then, you'll come to the Red Sea and snorkel with Bob and me." She throws her arm around Bob affectionately and says, "Married couples are the protectors and fully sanctioned escorts of single girls here in the Kingdom of Saudi Arabia."

"Gee. Thanks—that's a great offer. Camp Five, number 5350—unlatch the gate—then just ring the doorbell. I'll be ready and waiting. I don't want you to honk the horn—it just might wake a neighbor or draw the attention of security."

"We'll be there bright and early—say 6:30 sharp," Bob says.

Prayer time is over. I go into a crowded and noisy appliance store looking for Carolyn and Jan. I feel uncomfortable squeezing along narrow aisles brushing against men. I'm being pursued by heavily accented voices shouting prices in my face. The mixture of sweaty bodies, cigarettes, and hot breath nauseates me—not good on a stomach full of goat meat.

In this mayhem, I reach over a short man's shoulder and pull on Carolyn's sleeve. She turns and screams, "There's the Yankee from Ohio."

"Carolyn, let's get out of here!"

She denies my request and insists this store has the best prices and widest selection of electronics, appliances: anything you could want. Jan tags along passively. Carolyn does a swell job bartering with an aggressive salesman for a Sony tape deck and recorder that she thinks I should have. She saves me the equivalent of six dollars.

Next, she drags me to one of several stores dedicated solely to the sale of musical tapes. It's crowded as hell and louder than a rock concert. Since the tapes aren't labeled (only the jackets identify the artist) I suspect they are bootlegged. Carolyn takes over and grabs a bunch of tapes that she's sure I'll enjoy. I open my coin purse and she takes what she needs and completes the transaction.

We visit a few more stores jammed with imports and crowded with customers—a gold and brass shop among them. Besides the shops there are other vendors in the open-air market—scattered about haphazardly. They're selling clothing, sandals, dishes, and home furnishings besides food and beverages.

Carolyn, Jan, and I walk to where the white stretch limo is parked near the cars and trucks. The energy found in the crowded and noisy shops and the outdoor flea market is in stark contrast to the atmosphere surrounding the improvised parking lot that Carolyn says is called the "Love Park." There's a sadness in the air: slower movements, quieter voices, and a sense of longing for something more. We get back in the white stretch limo. Out the window, I watch some of my companions look over their shoulders and wave to their paramours.

Tonight I saw a group of men longing or maybe lusting after pretty young women. Likely, some of those needs were met this evening—here in a small town along the Red Sea in the Arabian Desert where mingling of the sexes is prohibited among single men and women. I think about Dan and wonder what I might have missed this evening.

The ride back to Camp Five is quiet—in contrast to the ride to old Yanbu. In anyone's language, or at least not in English or Tagalog, we didn't "paint the town red," or anything near it.

Chapter 7

Friday, September 18, 1987

My doorbell rings, I open the door.

"I'm happy to see you, Bev."

"Same here. It's very early, I know. But Bob insists all of our snorkeling adventures start at the crack of dawn so we can have the road to ourselves and enjoy our picnic before the sun becomes unbearable."

I climb in the back seat. "You two are not only my protectors and my escorts, but my rescuers. I was worried sick about how in the hell I was going to survive a day in the dungeon. I'm grateful to you both."

The Security guys watch as we pull away in a Nissan patrol at 6:30 a.m. on my first full day off work.

Bev says, "We may be rescuing you, but whoever we bring along provides us with a buffer. All ex-pat couples have strained marriages here in the Kingdom. They always make social plans for Friday. It's their only way to survive the tension and boredom. I'd kill Bob if he didn't drive us somewhere—anywhere."

Bob says, "We're going to swing by and pick up our friend, Dan."

"About Dan, if we get stopped, won't there be trouble? I'm only allowed to be with married couples. You know, the no mingling thing. Maybe I shouldn't go."

"I've heard that, but don't worry. The rules usually apply only to the others. They don't stop Westerners." Bob says, slowing the Nissan to a stop. Dan appears out of nowhere, and slips in beside me.

"Hey, everybody."

I'm tongue tied. His cologne is provocative. I recognize the scent, but can't name it, except to say it's divine. I want to ask him what it is he is wearing but I'm afraid my face will turn red.

It's 6:35 a.m. and we do have the road to ourselves. The barren desert is monotonous even though there are scads of abandoned cars along the way.

Bob says, "The abandoned cars are a result of three things. The typical Saudi driver is inexperienced, has developed poor driving habits—such as going too fast—and lacks the required know-how to repair cars. Camel breeding, they know. When you don't build the thing yourself, you can't know how to repair it—pretty much a result of sudden and untold wealth."

Bev claims to know little about the plight of single women ex-pats. I hesitate to get into a discussion about anything that has to do with the hospital because I haven't sorted it all out yet and I wouldn't want to be quoted, or, worse, misquoted on my impressions.

I turn my attention to Dan. "So, Dan, I'm here because of a layoff. At the hospital back in Ashtabula, Ohio, they called it 'restructuring.'"

He laughs and pats my hand. "I lost my job too—oil industry—Dallas. I've got a three-year old son to support, so in spite of the hardships here, I'm grateful to be employed. I can consistently and easily make my monthly child-support payments. I'm a technician at the refinery."

"How was the party last night?"

"You didn't miss much. But today, we're going to show you a good time."

I can't name the scent but I think it is made by Armani.

We are off the paved road now and I can't for the life of me figure how Bob could possibly know which direction we are headed in this featureless terrain. There's nothing around and I'm scared. The legendary image of a hostile, sun-seared, wind-scorched, waterless, endless desert, largely devoid of life, shelterless, with venomous creatures lurking under rocks, and a lone Bedouin on his camel prowling the most remote of the dry regions of the desert come to mind. Bev attempts to direct Bob's driving. He ignores her suggestions.

It seems dangerous and unnecessary for us to come all this way with only one vehicle. The Nissan could break down. What we really need here is a two-way radio and a lead car driven by an experienced Saudi. That other beach party that I'll be attending would make a good story to share with my three new best friends, but I'll keep it to myself for now.

Dan says, "I'm glad you joined the women's softball team. I enjoy coaching."

"I'll give it my best try."

"You've got the right bat and now you just need practice. Seriously, Kelly, once you're comfortable with the weapon and learn the proper grip, you'll be ready for the fundamentals of the swing."

"I won't be in the Kingdom that long."

"I'm going to see to it that you master the fundamentals of the swing."

"And they are?"

"Stance, stride, rotation, swing and most important, follow thru."

"Oh."

The sea that Moses parted over two thousand years ago appears before us. No cars, no crowds, no people at all, no beach umbrellas, no music boxes blaring, no signs of any kind to serve us notice that we have arrived at the edge of the sea—this is new for me—a trip to the seashore unspoiled by tourists, local crowds, or commercialism. No expanse of combed sun-bleached sand and pebbles. Now I know what unspoiled looks like—an uneven and rugged edge of shoreline, lumpy with rocks, stones, and sand. I like the look and feel of it.

Dear Bev and Bob are prepared with beach umbrellas, blankets, a picnic lunch, and snorkeling equipment for all of us. Thank God, Bev told me to wear my bathing suit under my blouse and jeans. There is no place to change. I feel so awkward getting out of my clothes—all of us stripping down together. Oh well. I'm glad to be wearing a modest one-piece suit and yet I still feel naked. We all look so naked. And as I anticipated, Dan has an impressive athletic body—no fat—all muscle.

Dan has decided to instruct me on snorkel equipment. It helped that I told him that I've never done this before and I don't know what to expect. He does a fine job of explaining and demonstrating the mask, snorkel, and fins. It's both awkward and exciting when he helps me put on the fins and adjust the mask on my face. I haven't felt this way in a long time.

He says, "I am going to hold your hand, just squeeze it if you become uncomfortable, and I'll bring you back safely to the shore."

Hand-in-hand we enter the warm waters of the Red Sea. I can't believe my eyes. We've entered a fairytale world. A panoramic and Technicolor world that's bursting with exquisite and exotic forms of all sizes, shapes, and stunningly beautiful colors in every gradation of hue and brightness—purples, reds, oranges, blues, blacks, whites, and on and on. I see little things that look like crabs, snails, tiny flowers, sponges, soft-bodied things and transparent tiny creatures. The abundance of creatures and plants—the movement and—the energy—dazzles and mesmerizes me. Dan dazzles me as well as he guides me with a squeeze of the hand or gentle tap on the shoulder.

Returning to the shore, we eat cold meat sandwiches and drink cans of Swan—a non-alcoholic beer from Australia. The four of us are mellowed out. The guys chat about contenders for division championships, and I say, "I'm an Indians fan. What's so funny about that?"

"Oh, that team, the farm team for the Yankees, right Dan?" Bob laughs.

"Kelly, you need to spend time in Texas, our state, the big state—not only the home of the Dallas Cowboys but also the glamorous setting for the best soap opera drama ever to come to TVland, the great Dallas," Bev boasts.

We chuckle, and Bev becomes more inspired. "On the other hand, no need to travel to the great state of Texas when we've got it all right here in this vast desert."

Bob looks at Dan and me and rolls his eyes.

Undaunted, Bev picks up the pace and raises the volume. "Our beloved sponsors who only want us to be safe, happy, content, and productive, while they prosper back home in the 'land of the free and home of the brave.' Faithfully, and I might add, in a timely manner, they overnight us the best games of the American and National leagues." And with her hand over her heart and head bowed, "our national past time," and then looking upward to the heavens, "and the icing on the cake is every single National Football League game."

Now lowering her voice, she speaks directly to me. "As an appeasement to the little aproned woman who tirelessly prepares home-cooked meals, does the washing and ironing, and yes, gets fucked twice a week—or maybe not fucked at all—every single precious thrilling episode of Dallas gets overnighted, too." She jumps up and starts to leave, turns back to her audience, smiles, and says, "Kelly, I'm not turning you off on marriage, am I?"

"Of course not, Bev."

"Let's wrap it up," says Bob. Dan and I get up and begin to help pack up. Heading back to town, I again thank Bev and Bob for inviting me. I tell Dan that he took me on a trip of a lifetime—wonderfully psychedelic. Dan squeezes my hand as he gets out of the Nissan. I'm relieved he is dropped off first. Then, I ask Bev to walk with me to my door because of the phobia. She agrees. The Security Patrol watches me exit the Nissan and enter the little courtyard at 5350 at 1:30 p.m., they are like bookends to my adventure to the red Sea.

.   .   .

Rising at 4:45 a.m. justifies a nap and will fill a block of time. There is nothing for me to do between now and work tomorrow morning. I can only write a letter or two and read for so long. The glorious morning at the Red Sea is something to write home about. But, if letters going out of the Kingdom are censored as Jan reports, I better not mention Dan. One of the best parts of the story will be missing. My new reality is a little warped.

I can't believe I slept for five hours straight. I'd clean the dungeon if I had cleaning supplies. I'd fix dinner if there was food in the dungeon. I'm hungry. The thought of walking all the way to the commissary and back is distasteful.

I'll need an escort. Fidelis doesn't answer her phone. Inger—no answer. Desperate times call for desperate measures. I call Jan and ask if she and Carolyn would like to join me on a trip to the commissary. I feel guilty using them as bodyguards as we weave our way through the maze. To assuage my guilt, I insist upon making dinner for the three of us. No argument from my bodyguards.

It's really kind of Jan and Carolyn to pretend that my feline phobia has nothing to do with me asking them to go to the commissary this evening. Sensitivity shown to a person with an outrageous neurotic phobia is a wonderful thing. So many people try to reason with me or argue me out of my craziness.

The three of us leave the commissary carrying overstuffed bags of groceries and head for 5350.

Jan and I unpack the bags of basics: cereal, milk, instant coffee, a two pound box of thin spaghetti, a large jar of a tomato based sauce, stuff for a salad, and a few cleaning supplies. While we're doing this in the narrow kitchen, Carolyn's unpacking last night's purchases of the tape deck and tapes. She shouts out, "What's your preference—Duran Duran, Phil Collins, Pet Shop Boys, Elton John, Annie Lennox?"

"You decide, please," I yell back.

Next thing we hear Carolyn alternating between reciting and singing selected lyrics from several songs. "So goodbye yellow brick road. Where the dogs of society howl ... Take, take me home, oh lord ... Cause I've been a prisoner all my life ..."

Jan whispers to me, "She's tone deaf, as you've just heard, but I haven't the heart to tell her. It gets worse. Wait until she does her Annie Lennox impersonation."

I laugh. This is fun—I'm glad they accepted my invitation.

"Let me fix the salad," Jan says as she's already lining up the ingredients on the pink formica countertop.

I grab a large pot from the cupboard, fill it with water, place it on the electric stovetop and flip the knob to high. In a smaller pot I dump the jar of sauce and flip the knob to low.

I poke my head into the living room and Carolyn's got a cigarette dangling from her lips, eyes closed, arms waving as she belts out, "Would I lie to you, would I lie to you, honey? Oh, no, no, no." I've never seen her so happy.

Back in the kitchen I dump the spaghetti noodles into the boiling water and stir the sauce. Jan is already setting the table in the dining area.

Our entertainer takes a break from singing, sticks her head in the kitchen, with sweat dripping from her chin, and cigarette in hand, she says, "What smells so good?"

"It's the oregano in the sauce," Jan says with authority from the dining area. "I worked as a cook in a diner all through my college days at Wayne State."

We sit at the table, then I jump up. "Sorry, I forgot the cans of Seven-Up."

"I've got something better," says Jan as she jumps up goes to her purse and brings a clear glass jar which contains about ten to twelve ounces of a colorless liquid. She unscrews the top, pours a few ounces in each of our glasses on the table.

"The best homemade gin you can get in Yanbu!"

"Oh my God, no! I mean, we shouldn't, what if we get caught? Just put it back—take it home." I feel so damn foolish. They just stare at me. "I mean, aren't you afraid?"

Carolyn laughs and says, "Once we swallow it, they can't find it."

Jan looks sullen and dejected and says nothing. She pours the gin from my glass back in the jar. Then both she and Carolyn snap open their cans of Seven-Up and pour it into their glasses. I feel so embarrassed—awkward. Carolyn takes her fork and stirs her gin and Seven-Up. Jan does the same. We eat in silence.

Unable to tolerate the chilly silence a minute longer, I say, "I apologize for the ordinary tomato and lettuce salad with the ordinary dressing, the plain dinner rolls, the off-the-shelf pasta sauce over basic spaghetti noodles, and the absence of dessert. I had no idea I'd be serving a former chef."

Jan says, "Really, everything is good."

"Brits don't eat fancy," Carolyn says and all three of us laugh.

There is no mention of the gin incident—like it never happened.

"I'll clear the table and load the dishwasher. Did I mention that I was the cook and sometimes the waitress and sometimes the dish washer at my uncle's diner in downtown Detroit?"

"Not exactly, Jan," I smile at her. "I'll be your assistant."

Carolyn joins us in the narrow kitchen with cigarette in hand. "I'll brew us a spot of tea."

I look at her, hang my head in shame and say, "No tea, I'm all out. Will instant coffee do?"

She takes a long drag on the cigarette, blows the smoke out with her mouth pointed up towards the ceiling. "Yes, thank you. I'll take it black, please." She spins around and almost knocks me over as she bolts from the kitchen.

Jan whispers, "She didn't make it in drama school, so she became a mid-wife instead." I chuckle and observe that Jan enjoys Carolyn's wacky ways.

Again, we're sitting at the table. Carolyn stares into her coffee cup. Finally, she says, "I've made a bit of a mess of things." Jan clears her throat. I feel chilly. I get up and turn off one of the air-conditioners.

"What's wrong, Carolyn?" I ask.

Tears flow. Jan gets up and fetches tissues from her purse, places them in Carolyn's hand and puts her arm around Carolyn's shoulder. Carolyn dries her tears and says, "I haven't saved but a few hundred pounds. Can't do any of the things I've dreamed of doing for myself or my family. I can't go home empty-handed." She further confesses that she's squandered more money on silly junk, gold jewelry, and tons on long distance phone calls, and blown money when on leave to London showing off for her friends.

Jan says, "You're not the only one who has done that. Come on, we both know others who have done the very same thing. Spent like crazy. That's why Poey remains here. She's ashamed to return home without a bankroll."

More tears fall. Carolyn says, "The truth is I took all my gold to London and sold every last piece of it. Then I partied with my friends. I wasn't mugged or robbed. I'm just broke."

The three of us are sad as we say good night.

I feel I should call the Bruces and tell them how thankful I am for the wonderful excursion this morning. I should call Dan too and thank him for his support, which truly made my first snorkeling adventure something very special, but I am too sad to talk right now and it's after nine already.

After the adventure this morning, I thought I just might be able to handle this experience. But, as nice as Dan is, it would be foolish to get involved. It seems that some ex-pats are driven or provoked to make poor choices due to feelings of deprivation or whatever. I wonder how I might behave after six months of restrictions and having to sneak around—watch my back—so to speak.

I shower and go to bed but I can't sleep. It's 11:30. I hear cats. Damn it.

I get out of bed and go to the living area. The creepy noise seems to be coming from the side yard. I open the drapes covering the sliding glass doors. It's very dark out there. I move closer to the glass door, lean forward, squint, stare, look right and left. A light shines in my direction. I flinch. A bunch of cats run across the small shrubless dirt yard enclosed by a low stack of bricks. I see a man out there beyond the bricks. He has on a white shirt. He stands bold and motionless and holds a gigantic flashlight.

Acid squirts up from my stomach to my throat and burns like hell. I pick up the telephone receiver and my sweaty hand drops it on the floor. Where are the damn emergency numbers? Of course, posted on the kitchen wall while the phone is in the living room. The instructions are laced with misspelled words, numbers crossed out and others written in. In the event of a fire, go to Line A; in the event of a flood, go to Line C; if after midnight, call the second number. I go back to the living room, pick the receiver from the floor and dial the hospital.

"Moktar, please, please come quickly. There's a man in my yard." What is he doing operating the switchboard? Who the hell cares? I'm damn glad it was him. I glance over my shoulder—the man and the bright light remain. I'm so scared. I need to get out of view. I tip-toe to the front door as though tip-toing would make a difference in this craziness. I pray, please God, keep me safe from harm. I'm so sorry for all of my past sins.

There's a banging on the door. I check the peephole and let Moktar in. I grab his upper arm and pull him towards the glass doors. "there —see out there to the left."

"Stay here, lock the door." His manner is definite. I stand near the front door—out of the sight of the man in the white shirt.

The doorbell rings—once—then again. I hear male voices. I check the peephole—the faces of two guys.

"Who is it?"

"Security."

"Come in." I think to myself, how dumb and trusting can I be.

The two men dressed in Security uniforms enter—we stand in the center of the living room.

"What happened?" the shorter one asks with a poker face.

I'm so relieved that he speaks English. I point to the glass doors. "A light, a man over there to the left. At first I heard cats." I hear myself say "cats" and it makes me sick. Cats are everywhere for God's sake.

What the hell does that have to do with a man in my yard flashing a light in my apartment? The men look at each other.

The short one shrugs his shoulders and talks to the taller one, in Arabic, for what seems like forever. It can't take that long to repeat my fragmented story which included only one extraneous fact. They both look perplexed.

The doorbell rings. I jump, check the peephole, and let Moktar in.

"Everything is okay, Kelly." He turns to the two guys and they all talk at once in Arabic. I bet the three of them think I'm crazy. Finally, Moktar turns to me and says, "There were two men fixing a broken water pipe. They finished and are gone now."

"But why the light turned into my apartment?"

"It's okay now, Kelly."

"Are you sure"

"Are you all right? Do you need to go to the hospital?"

"Of course not."

Moktar talks to the guys again in Arabic, and all three of them begin to check the windows in the kitchen, bedroom, bath, spare room, and the sliding glass doors. I stand in the living room. Oh my God, Jan's goddamn jar of gin sits on the coffee table. She must have forgotten it. Surely, she didn't plant it here. Paranoia rears its ugly head.

"Are you okay, Kelly?"

"Moktar, I'm fine, really. Fine."

I nod to the short one and then the tall one, and I let them out.

I skillfully maneuver Moktar towards the dining area in order to avoid the jar of gin on the coffee table and ask him if he'd like coffee. He accepts, and I suggest that we sit at the dining room table. I'm acutely aware that I am entertaining a Saudi male, who is married at that—just the two of us. He explains that two men did work on fixing a water pipe and that one of them likely wandered to get a peek into an apartment.

I tell him about my trip to the Red Sea today. He says some evenings he takes his wife and kids to the sea and when it gets dark, they build a fire and count the stars in the sky.

We've run out of small talk—our coffee cups are empty. I walk him to the door. I'd love to hug him or at least shake his hand, but I'll have to be satisfied with our chat over coffee. I wouldn't dream of mentioning the switchboard, and for now, I never plan to. I say good night and he says, "Inshallah."

I pick up the jar from the coffee table, take it to the kitchen sink, remove the lid, and recall the first time I had a gin and tonic on my twenty-first birthday in the company of my parents at my uncle's restaurant. I remember I enjoyed the taste and the feeling of adulthood. I guzzle the gin.

Chapter 8

Saturday, September 19, 1987

"Good morning, Fidelis."

"What's wrong, Kelly? You look terrible?"

"I had a terrible, terrible night—I got three hours sleep tops."

I tell Fidelis about the broken water pipe—Peeping Tom—Moktar —security guys. But, I don't tell her about the gin.

"What do you think? Please, I need your honest feedback. I'm losing perspective on everything."

"It's true water pipes break. And that's easy enough for me to check on," she smiles, "the Filipino network."

"Peeping Toms?"

She hesitates, "Yes, unfortunately they do occur—Camp Five—a haven for those types."

"I remember Carolyn prattling about them—I didn't take her seriously."

"Think about it, Kelly. Male ground-keepers, male repairmen, male twenty-four hour security patrol and a little colony of women who have dared to learn a trade and leave home. Camp Five is a magnet for all types of curious men."

"Fidelis, that's interesting—I never thought of it like that. Your use of the word 'curious' is exceedingly polite. It's sort of like we're a circus—Circus Five. Really, we're all looking at each other here. The Women's Room at the airport, the Women and Children swimming pool—even in Old Yanbu—we all looked each other over. Question is —when does the dialogue begin?"

Fidelis shrugs her shoulders.

. . .

Khaled, Dr. Small, Rick, and I gather in the conference room. Khaled announces that Rashid Zahran from corporate headquarters will be here late this afternoon. Khaled will meet with him first, then me. Next, Dr. Small will take him on a tour of the clinical areas. After that, Rick will take him around to the non-clinical areas.

I notice perspiration on Khaled's brow, and I say, "This sounds ominous."

"Miss Day is correct. It spoiled my weekend. It's not a good sign. I was informed by fax on Thursday as I was leaving here."

"What do you think it's about? I mean something must be up ... I'd think," says Dr. Small as his hand goes to his ear.

Khaled heaves a huge sigh. "Well, midwives for one. Carolyn Thomas's replacement reneged on her contract. Actually there were two midwives expected—both reneged."

"I couldn't deliver a baby to save my soul. We're gonna be in a real jam, I think," says Dr. Small, now dabbing his ear with his handkerchief. The bleeding appears to be out of control. I vividly recall the ear, the picking, and scales of dead skin upon our first meeting and now blood. "I've got an ulcer. I wish my wife would hurry up and get here."

"Is it true that Carolyn is as competent as I've heard? My source, of course, is Carolyn."

"Kelly, I'd let her deliver my grandchildren. Yes, yes, I would. I mean, I think I would," claims Dr. Small.

Khaled says, "I made rounds very early this morning and found a number of things out of order." His face is grim, the flabby jowls are not swaying. "I found a posting on the employee bulletin board requesting a locum wife."

Rick snickers. Dr. Small's tiny green eyes get bigger. Khaled explains that locum means a temporary position. He gives an example: the person would fill the position of a person who is on holiday. Mainly this is used for critical, essential employees, such as physicians and pharmacists.

The room is quiet. Then Dr. Small volunteers, "I'll, I'll have a talk with the guy ... write him a warning memo."

"Please do," says Khaled. "Werner, the pharmacist is the offender, and he requires a strong warning."

Rick looks up from his doodling and over at me. I look away. His propensity to snicker and make fun can be hilarious but not what we need right now.

Khaled continues with a long list of infractions: inadequate partitions separating males from females, loud laughing, employee name badges clipped at the waist—not up near the neck where they should be, and mismanagement of the Holy Koran, among other things.

Then he says, "Angelita will re-circulate the directive on the Holy Koran. The hospital has several copies and we want to make them available to the Muslim patients. This book is very sacred, and it must be properly safeguarded. Only Muslim patients and Muslim hospital personnel are permitted to touch and handle it. I have designated Moktar responsible for their control and distribution. I must caution everyone that any mismanagement in this procedure may subject the employee involved to disciplinary action."

"Has there been a problem, Khaled, with mishandling of the Holy Koran?" I ask.

"Yes, about eight months ago, when I first arrived here, we had a problem of non-Muslims holding the Holy Koran copies and looking through them, and this is not acceptable to us. We want to avoid this from happening again. Please visit your departments and make sure things are in order. We must tighten things up around here."

Rick grits his teeth and Dr. Small is doing the ear thing again. The meeting is over.

I ask Mr. Al Kahairi for a few minutes of his time and follow him to his office. I propose that we allow Carolyn to go on a month-to-month contract to fill the gap until we get more midwives on board. Mr. Al Kahairi screws up his face and shoves a candy into his mouth. He pushes three pieces of candy across the desk towards me.

"Carolyn is free to go next Saturday. I plan to tell her today. She hates it here. She's been screaming about getting out of here ever since she went to the police about a mugger. She won't stay on. Corporate is on me about the Irish midwives who reneged on their contracts. We need midwives badly."

"If I get her to stay, do you think the mugging and robbery incident could be put to rest?"

He looks surprised and says, "Get her to stay."

I call Carolyn and ask her to join me at the Pizza Palace for lunch right after the noon prayer. She agrees but asks if Jan can join us. I tell her it's really about her status here, but if she's sure she wants Jan to be privy to her business, it's okay with me.

I phone the Pizza Place and place an order for a large pizza with everything on it and tell them we'll be there shortly after prayer time. I start to mull over the events of yesterday from the delightful Red Sea adventure, Carolyn's financial problems, the Peeping Tom, Moktar's kindness and the gin incident. This place is not without drama.

Carolyn and Jan join me at the Pizza Palace. "Let's get right down to business."

"Sure," says Carolyn.

"As you well know, Carolyn, we're short of midwives. You've been very generous in giving us a lot of overtime. By the way, Dr. Small admires your work. I'd like you to stay on." I sit back in my chair.

Carolyn puts her slice of pizza back on her plate, leans forward. "But that bloody King Khaled—he hates me—he won't ..."

Jan interrupts her by placing her hand on Carolyn's forearm. "Let Kelly finish," she says. Carolyn sits back in her chair and folds her hands on her lap. Jan returns to her pizza pleased with herself for not only giving Carolyn direction, but that Carolyn follows her direction.

"Mr. Al Kahairi is on board." I can't believe Carolyn's speechless, but she is. "We need your skills. The mugging and robbery thing—just drop it—move on."

Jan says, "I'll help you. I'll monitor your spending, make a budget for you, and in no time you'll have savings."

"And I'll monitor your drinking," Carolyn high-fives Jan and me.

On the way back to the hospital, I say to Carolyn, "You've got a good friend here in Jan and I'm glad you joined us."

. . .

Steve sticks his head in the doorway to my office. "I told you, Miss Kelly, Moktar has a frightful amount of clout around here. He's an expert on the rules of the Kingdom—knows when and how to bend them. He's awfully savvy when dealing with Security, and I might add he rescues damsels in distress in the wee hours of the night. 'Tis grand to know him—awfully swell old chap."

I feel my face get red. He tickles me. "Steve, do you know every-thing? You think you're smart don't you? You probably already know this but Lady Laila is being discharged today. So maybe that issue will just fade away."

"You mean swept under the tent, as we say here in the Kingdom? By Jove, I bet it will."

He wanders off and Angelita sticks her head in my office.

"The sitting room down the hall—he's waiting for you," she smiles.

The door to the sitting room is open and Mr. Rashid Zahran is standing looking out the picture window which faces a courtyard, just like the one in my office. I tap on the open door. He turns and indi-cates a chair for me. He closes the door to this small but comfortable and well-lit room. Mr. Rashid Zahran is of average height, medium build, wearing the traditional loose white robe, and white flowing head cover. His posture is stiff as he sits erect and almost motionless except for massaging a string of blue crystal beads that he holds in his left hand. I wouldn't describe him as handsome, but he's got the kind of face you like to rest your eyes on. I'm guessing late twenties.

"Miss Day, I realize that you just started—but I was wondering about your first impressions of the hospital."

"Well, my impressions are probably things you already know."

"Tell me anyway."

"Our primary business is delivering babies. The newborns are generally healthy. The next big business is the ER—car accident victims mainly, busiest in the evenings. Otherwise, very routine stuff. The patients on the wards are not very sick. The population in this new town is young and healthy. I rarely see an old person here at the hospital or on the street."

"Right. Do you think the hospital could handle a disaster?"

"Good question and an important one as well. Ask me that the next time we meet."

"Fair enough." He smiles for the first time. Come to think of it, I haven't smiled yet.

"Miss Day, you are entitled to R&R at the completion of your first two months. Let's see, that would be early November. I bring this up because it's good to take a break—especially when it's your first experience in the Kingdom. Any thoughts about where you'd like to go?"

"No, really, actually I haven't completely unpacked yet." Now I smile. He talks about London and Bangkok and friends and connections for a while. Then he stops. I guess it's my turn.

"London—Bangkok—something to think about." Brilliant comeback, Kelly.

"Some Saudi men have different ideas about freedom in the West," says Mr. Zahran. "They think all you have to do is ask a woman for sex … They haven't traveled abroad. They're not educated."

"Are you saying you're not like them?" Oops, I made him blush.

He says, "With respect to attitudes about women, I am not like them. Miss Day, I wish you a pleasant stay in Yanbu. If you should decide to go to London or Bangkok, have Angelita put us in touch, and I will give you my contacts."

"Thank you." He intrigues me. He's stilted, shy, awkward. Not nearly as sexy or smooth as Dan, yet I find him seductive. His quiet reserve is attractive.

.   .   .

Poor, nervous Dr. Small appears in my office. "How did it go? What's his mood?"

"You mean Mr. Zahran, I presume."

"Yes, yes, of course."

I begin to tell him. He begins to scratch his already badly excoriated ear.

"He was very pleasant. He explained that Saudi men who haven't traveled outside the Kingdom or have not had the benefit of an education think all they have to do is ask a Western woman for sex, and it's his for the taking. He talked about London and Bangkok. He wished me a pleasant stay in Yanbu. Actually, he's a rather attractive guy. You'll like him. Do you know anything about him?"

Dr. Small's green eyes get big, he whispers, "Arab elite, royal born, big deal, so they say."

I'm taken aback when, with a devilish grin he adds, "I think he's got King Khaled shitting bricks."

I laugh so hard I cry. While I continue to cry, he continues to talk.

"Wish me luck. I'm up next to do a walk through. I wish my wife were here. I forgot why I came here."

Struggling to compose myself, I say, "You came in here to find out about my meeting with Mr. Zahran."

I visit my areas to see if there are any problems/concerns/anxieties about Mr. Zahran's visit. You can hear a pin drop in the ER. Nothing is going on. I look for Steve and I find him in the break room munching on a big chocolate donut.

"Steve, come out in the hall and talk to me."

"Come in here, I'll share this with you. Coffee?"

"No, thanks. Please come out in the hall or nurses' station, so we can talk."

He jumps up from the table, carrying the donut and coffee cup.

"I want to be sure you know Mr. Zahran from the corporate office is visiting us as we speak."

"I know. Moktar told me. He's top camel, you know. Mr. Zahran, I mean. He's their new 'Wonder Boy'—educated in the United States of America—the best and the brightest—Harvard."

"Are things in order here?"

"Tiptop shape." He grins, licks chocolate off his fingers, and says, "I'm planning a smashing party and I want to extend a special invitation to My Lady."

"Steve, please stop this nonsense of party planning. We've got Mr. Zahran here on a mission. Make sure staff keep their voices down, are prominently displaying their identification badges, and are not mingling or showing too much skin."

I go to each nursing area and repeat my spiel. Then I return to my office. I pull a Snicker's candy bar from my purse and wonder how long it (the candy bar) took to get here and by what route. Sitting at my desk, I stare at the postage stamp, chew on the stale bar and think about the concept of separation of church and state. I've taken it for granted all my life. I've never thought of or imagined living life in any other way. I didn't know there was another way. I like the distance between organized religion and national state. But then that's what I grew up with. I want to mingle with the opposite sex. I'd like to go to the parties—that's what I'm used to. But here and now in this place the law prohibits me from going to parties and mingling.

Dr. Small sticks his head in my office. "Oh, Kelly, I told Mr. Zahran that you think he's an attractive guy."

"You what?"

"Well, you said ..."

"Damn it, Dr. Small, how could you? Did you say anything else about me and what I think?"

"No, no, that was all, I think. Don't be mad, Kelly."

I grab my purse and plan to link up with Fidelis and walk to 5350 but my phone rings.

"Kelly," Angelita says, "Fidelis had an emergency and she won't be available to go to the softball game tonight."

"Is there anything I can do? Is there something wrong?"

"I'm so busy, I can't talk now, Kelly."

What the hell. I know something is wrong. Everything was okay this morning. Now what? I walk to Fidelis's office and as I expected she's not there. My heart sinks.

. . .

It's early evening and about eighty degrees. I walk to the Saudi Turf with the Louisville Slugger under my arm. I'm bundled up for modesty in a loose, red, long-sleeved shirt and baggy blue jeans. I reminded myself that Fidelis said softball is a healthy diversion—survival kit material. I miss her.

Bob does a roll call and doles out team assignments. I tell him I don't know when Fidelis will return. I'm assigned to the Stoned Sands, Dan's team. Inger goes to the Royal Oils, and no surprise, Rick is the coach. Interestingly, Bev is on the Bedouin Babes, and Bob's their coach. Fidelis would be on the Smokin' Camels if she were here.

After fifteen minutes of warm up exercises, my very first softball game gets under way. Sands play Oils. My first at bat and I'm facing Inger. I'm nervous. I'm thinking—stance—stride and I hear, "Ball one," shouted out from I don't know where. The catcher admonishes me—"Pay attention—look at the ball." Swing—miss, swing—miss, swing—miss. Out I am. It's my turn again—so soon already. I actually hit the ball—I can't believe it—I run as fast as I can—tagged out only half-way to first. Out of breath and with severe pain in both thighs, I trudge to the bench.

I stand in the right field—sometimes I move forward and sometimes backwards. Nothing comes my way. Oils are up by two runs.

My turn at bat again. Strike one, strike two. I watch for the ball, I see it coming. I hit it so hard that I hear a smacking sound. The ball doesn't go out of the park—for an instant I thought it might—but I make it safely to first. Maybe I can develop some skills.

Game over. Oils over Sands 6-3. We watch the Babes and Camels finish their game. Our coaches join us. Rick wallows in the praise of the Oils victory. Inger complains that hitting a long ball and running around the bases has completely exhausted her. Dan tells the Sands that we played well and he looks forward to Monday evening's game. He takes me aside and says, "You look sharp in red."

I laugh and say, "Thanks, it's my lucky shirt."

"How about if I call you sometime?"

"Yes, you may." I think of Fidelis' words of caution that now is not the time or place to fall in love. While we're chatting I see the white-stretch limo pull away. I wanted to take it because my legs really hurt. "Good night, Dan, I need to get going."

I join Inger and Rick and say, "We should be going, Inger."

"Kelly, Rick and I want to celebrate the win tonight." Rick grins.

"Kelly, we'll drop you off."

"I can't take the risk. Security often parks by my unit. Inger, I think you're crazy to take such a big chance. Are you never afraid?"

"We're going to the married camp—remember—Rick's house sitting."

"Okay, you two. You're on your own and I'm on my own. See you tomorrow morning."

This is my first time walking to Camp Five alone in the evening. I don't like it already. I should have asked Bev and Bob for a ride—after all, they're married, albeit unhappily. My legs hurt, I'm so tired, I'd like to walk quickly but I can't—I'm too sore. The Louisville Slugger weighs more than it should as I drag it along. Into Camp Five I go. My heart rate picks up. Security is parked near 5350. I look to see if the security guy in the car could possibly be one of the guys from last night—I'll take my chances and ask for help. No luck. I don't think I've ever seen that guy before. When I return to Ashtabula, I will see a psychiatrist and get over the damn phobia.

I stand near the wooden gate. Stretch my arm straight out in front of me with bat clutched tightly. I step nearer to the gate, hold my breath and poke the gate with the end of the bat. Nothing happens. I poke again. I poke harder this time and nothing happens. I close in and unlatch the gate. Coast clear. I rush to open the door. I'm inside. This is no way to live.

I dial Fidelis's number—let it ring twenty-five times. I open a can of diet Seven-Up, sit at the table and try to distract myself with thoughts of Dan—the snorkeling, his compliments tonight, and his interest in me. All is well and good—but where's Fidelis? I'll try her number again tomorrow morning. On the plus side, Carolyn is staying—at least for a while and I got a base hit tonight, and unlike last night—no Peeping Tom—so far. I could use a shot of gin in this Seven-Up.

Chapter 9

Sunday, September 20, 1987

I'm ready for work. I dial Fidelis's number and let it ring and ring and ring. I'm worried about her. The cats—I grab the Louisville Slugger. I'll use it to shoo the cats away if necessary. Like lightning, I'm out the door, through the courtyard and on the street. I notice the garbage can standing outside my courtyard. It is a formidable sight. That's odd. It's usually equidistant between my unit and the next unit. Cats and garbage cans go hand in hand. I miss Fidelis.

I feel silly walking to the hospital with a bat in hand. I put the Louisville Slugger in a corner of my office, throw my purse in the lower desk drawer, wipe my sweaty face with a tissue and head for the conference room.

Close behind me, Rick drags himself into the conference room looking a lot hungover, with breath to prove it as he sits next to me and says, "happy Sunday morning my fellow Americans—aren't we supposed to be in church?"

Dr. Small laughs and says, "I wish I were anywhere sitting with my wife listening to a good preacher. I mean not that I mind this but ..."

Khaled enters without a greeting and before he sits down, says, "He, Mr. Zahran, wants us to prepare a report." The three of us wait patiently for something more from Khaled. But, as expected, Dr. Small's anxiety overtakes him.

"What, what are you ah, they, he talking about—I mean there are all kinds of reports?"

"Look at this laundry list he gave me." Khaled passes around a copy of the list to each of us. We study it.

Again, Dr. Small speaks up, "Golly, I'm a doctor, not an MBA. This stuff is a little out of my league." The fingers move to the ear.

Rick says, "My information systems department, as small as it is, generates tons of reports—enough data to clog the Suez Canal."

"Rick, do you—when can you give us these reports or at least a list of them?" Khaled asks.

"All I need is fifteen to twenty minutes and a wheelbarrow."

"Please, let's meet back here," looking at his watch, "say at ten? Thanks, everyone."

I follow Rick out. "Can we talk for just a minute?"

Against the rules, I close my office door. "Rick, what do you think is going on?"

"I think the whole thing is bizarre. Something is going on. I just didn't know what. Wonder Boy from Harvard can't be here about name badges and silly shit. How about that please and thanks from King Khaled? Suspicious—to use one of his favorite words."

I chuckle, "We're on the same page. Let's talk more later, Rick."

When the team returns to the conference room at ten, computer print-outs are piled high on the table. Rick presents a tentative work plan and time table to meet Wonder Boy's request. He gives Khaled a list of questions to fax to Mr. Zahran. Rick explains that faxing is preferred to phoning so we won't have to answer any of Zahran's questions if he should have any at this time. Dr. Small is fretting and scratching. As we each gather up our printouts, Dr. Small says, "By the way, Fidelis left yesterday to accompany Carmencita back to the Philippines."

"What? She never said anything … "

"It was a last minute thing, Kelly. I mean it really was."

"Did you know about this, Mr. Al Kahairi?" I ask.

He looks to Dr. Small and says nothing. Dr. Small says, "Kelly, it was a last minute decision."

Looking anxious, Khaled says, "let's regroup at 2:30 and see where we stand."

. . .

I go to my office. I'm confused. Something is fishy. Why Fidelis? It was my understanding a nurse would accompany someone who's had a nervous breakdown—not the chief of housekeeping. Dr. Small seemed uneasy. But then, he always does. I pick up the phone and call Moktar and ask him to come to my office.

"Have a seat, Moktar. Tell me please, do you know anything about Fidelis accompanying Carmencita back to the Philippines?"

"I took them to the airport. It was on short notice. Usually, I know about airport trips a day or two in advance. That is all I know."

"Fidelis said nothing to me about this. I mean absolutely nothing. Something is not right. I just start to relax—think just maybe I could survive a year—then something happens, and I have so many doubts." He's a good listener. I sigh and change the conversation. "Tell me about the Muslim religion."

He smiles, crosses his long legs, leans back in the chair. "Allah is the Islamic name for God. One who worships Allah believes in the teachings of Islam. All the teachings, rules—all of it, are contained in the Koran, the Islamic Holy Book." He pauses. He looks around the room like he's gathering up his thoughts.

"Tell me more."

His tone is serious and thoughtful as he continues. "Five rules are prescribed duties for all devout Muslims: professing faith—repeating the Muslim creed; praying five times daily; giving alms; fasting; and making a pilgrimage to Mecca—Mohammed's birthplace—at least once in a lifetime. That's if you're able. You're smiling, Kelly."

"Sounds very familiar." I share with him that I was baptized Catholic. That we believe in prayer also, fasting during Lent, going to church regularly, pilgrimages to holy places—Vatican city, that is our big destination. But unlike most religions we confess our sins to a priest."

Moktar smiles and says, "I've heard about that."

"I've had twelve years of Catholic schooling. Religions have more in common than they have differences, don't you agree?"

He nods.

"When are you going to make that pilgrimage?"

"That pilgrimage was made with my parents and eight older brothers—I was a very young boy—it's my favorite family memory. It brings me peace every time I recall that holy place."

"Okay, one more question. When you go to the mosque, what do you pray about? Do you ask for anything—miracles—good health—a winning lottery ticket?"

He looks surprised, laughs, and says, "No, no requests. We praise Allah and we thank Him."

"So praise and gratitude it is."

"Yes."

He gets up from the chair, hesitates as though he's deciding what to say. I wait. I see frown lines on his face for the first time. He leaves. It seems as though he changed his mind about saying something. No one will ever convince me that he's a bad guy.

I shut the door, gaze out the picture window, and stare at the red flowers on the little bush for a minute or two. Life is strange. Then I organize myself at my desk, wink at the postage stamp that leans against the base of the desk lamp, and dive into a stack of computer printouts.

It's 11:30, and I have had enough for now. I stand up and stretch. The phone rings—it's Dr. Small. He wants to go to lunch with me— the Pizza Palace. It seems he knows my routine.

We walk to the Pizza Palace, and he says "I think we can pull off sitting together." He chuckles and says, "After all, we could be husband and wife for all they know."

"I really doubt that, Dr. Small. I've got an idea. We'll order separately, pay separately, and sit at separate tables. When they close up for prayer time, we'll sit together." He smiles and nods in agreement. The plan works. We sit together for twenty minutes and I learn a few things about Homer. He asks me to call him that.

"I grew up in rural Kansas on a farm—roped steers, herded cattle, attended county fairs and rodeos." He's relaxed and seems proud as he reminisces about the early mornings and hard work. I notice for the first time that he has huge, strong-looking hands and broad shoulders.

His broad shoulders slump and his voice becomes softer. "My brother died in a bizarre tractor accident, and my parents never really recovered from their loss. They encouraged me to go to college and on to medical school." He laments. "I did what they wanted. I felt guilty about my big brother's death and felt sorry for my parents." He stares down at the pizza, then he looks at me. I put my slice of pizza back on my plate.

"When I finished my residence in family practice, I married Constantia—she was a medical transcriber at the time. I never enjoyed medical practice, so I switched to hospital administration, and I don't like it either. Truth be told, I'd rather be twisting balloons into animals."

We sit quietly, then I ask, "Any children?"

"Yes, James, our only child. Let's see, he's twenty-five now and lives in San Francisco. He's gay and Constantia says all she ever wanted in life was a daughter and grandchildren." He says, "I love my son."

He turns the subject to work. "You'd think I'd know something about the workings of a hospital pharmacy, being a doctor and all, but I don't. I've had two meetings with Werner, he's our pharmacist, who wants a locum wife."

I smile. "I remember that incident and how perturbed Khaled was."

"But anyhow, the meetings with him weren't that helpful. Actually, after spending time with him, I thought—does he even know what he's doing?"

"Maybe I can help. I dated the Chief Pharmacist at Ashtabula General for one long boring year—don't ask me why. I learned more than I wanted to know about running a hospital pharmacy."

We walk back to the hospital and go to his office. I look over his notes from the brief meetings he had with Werner and some printouts. At first pass, it appears Werner doesn't manage his inventory very well. I make a list of questions that we'll need to ask him. We go to the pharmacy, ring the bell and wait. Ring it again and again. Finally, Werner appears and buzzes us into his work area.

"What do you need?" His piercing blue eyes narrow.

"May we have a look at the narcotic log book?" I ask.

"It's right over there on the shelf," he points and continues the task at hand with his back towards us.

Then we ask him to unlock a closet. He does. We thank him and leave and go back to Dr. Small's office. Some things just don't add up. Either Werner is incompetent or a thief—maybe both.

Promptly at 2:30, we assemble in the conference room. Dr. Small starts off by laying out the discrepancies discovered in the pharmacy. There are narcotics not accounted for and a huge overstock of antibiotics. Record keeping is sloppy at best. Fraudulent record keeping is suspected as well.

Khaled expresses concern that he was the one responsible for hiring Werner. Dr. Small tugs at his ear and complains that he's Werner's supervisor.

Rick says, "Don't worry we've uncovered something here, and this is important. I'll call Rashid Zahran and brief him on this finding and he can get the corporate office involved."

We all agree that it should be dealt with now. Rick goes to his office to make the call to Mr. Zahran.

Dr. Small says he doesn't feel good. Khaled excuses himself and says he'll be back in a few minutes. Dr. Small says, "Kelly, do you think Werner suspects we're on to something?"

"I don't know—it's possible."

"If he's got something to hide … I'm having chest pain, Kelly."

"It can't hurt to check it out." I walk him slowly down the corridor and into the ER where, between Steve and Jan, he's hooked up to a heart monitor in a matter of seconds. Stat blood work and a chest x-ray are ordered.

"Likely a case of indigestion," Jan whispers in my ear.

Rick, Khaled, and I, along with Angelita, find each other in cubicle six in the ER at Dr. Small's bedside. He'll be transferred to the tele-metry unit in just a few minutes for twenty-four hour observation. Jan assures us that he's going to be okay.

Rick brings Khaled and me up to date. Mr. Zahran, along with the pharmacy liaison from the corporate office, will be on the first flight out of Jeddah tomorrow morning, due at the hospital around 9:00. We're to take a business as usual attitude until then. They'll surprise Werner. Meanwhile, Werner can't go anywhere because the hospital has his passport. We move on to a discussion of other areas of the hospital and find ourselves winding up things at 6:00 p.m.

We're dog-tired. The three of us take a peek in at Dr. Small and note that he's sleeping comfortably. Rick volunteers to drive me home. Khaled says that he should because he's in a better position to explain in the event that Security stops us. Khaled drives me to 5350. I go to get out of the car, and he says, "Let me check for cats first." He never asked me why I was carrying a bat.

My phone is ringing off the hook as I enter 5350.

Bev and Bob invite me to join them and Dan for an evening cook-out under the stars at a beach along the Red Sea this evening. "Sounds fabulous, I'm truly flattered that you thought of me, but I am afraid … that mingling thing … I'm sad to say I pass."

"Kelly, please come. I want you to come. I'll even sit in the back seat with you and the guys will be up front," she pleads.

"I can't, I'm chicken, sorry, really," I whine.

Within minutes the phone rings again.

"Kelly, I want you to reconsider the invitation. Bev, Bob and I talked. Bob is a big deal at Aramco and he is a westerner, an American. That's a lot of clout. Nobody is going to bother him."

I listen. "Call me or Bev if you change your mind. We'll depart in the next fifteen minutes and I promise we'll have you back by curfew."

"You're funny. But, I'm firm on this."

He insists I take down his phone number, and that of Bev and Bruce.

I think about fixing supper. I think about Fidelis. I pick up the phone and dial.

"Hello, Dan. I've changed my mind."

I climb into the back seat of the Nissan Patrol next to Bev. The guys chat about football and the potential ramifications of the NFL players strike.

We're on the outskirts of town, and I see a strange sight. "What was that?" I ask my companions.

"You haven't seen an outdoor coffeehouse? Bev asks.

"Nope."

"Bob, slow down at the next coffeehouse so Kelly can get a good look."

Bob explains, "These are cafes where men smoke. It's a social thing and very popular in the Arab world. It's kinda like guys hanging out at a bar but smoking, not drinking. It's an ancient custom. We'll soon pass another one—these are outdoor, but they can be indoors as well."

"Do you know about a hookah—also known as a water pipe?" Dan asks me.

"No, not really."

He laughs. "You've never been in a drug paraphernalia shop back home?"

"No again. So, enlighten me."

"There's a lot of different types, but mainly you have a mouthpiece, a connecting flexible tube, a water bowl, and a vase. We're coming up to one now. Bob slow down so Kelly can get a look."

Next to a gas station surrounded by parked pickup trucks and cars is something that resembles an old style college dormitory—but in the open air. Men in white robes and traditional headdresses are reclining on what looks like old army cots but much higher off the ground. A hookah is on a stand next to the cot.

Bob says, "shisha is what they're smoking. In some areas, shisha is restricted in public and only available indoors—in coffeehouses and only on the outskirts of town. In Jeddah, shisha is not restricted at all. It's available in the city and outskirts—so they say."

Bev chimes in, "You can buy a hookah in the market at Yanbu's old town."

We arrive at our destination and unload the van.

"Kelly and I will comb the beach for firewood," Dan volunteers.

He takes my hand and leads me closer to the rolling sea. A soft breeze blows. I can smell Dan's cologne. A huge early evening sky plays host to a pure orange sun setting on the horizon.

"This is absolutely magnificent—it's so perfect and peaceful. Thank you for encouraging me to come along."

Dan grins and says, "My pleasure."

If he decides to kiss me, I'll be a willing participant for sure. If he doesn't, I'll be disappointed for sure. I should give him some kind of a signal, a green light, so to speak. I need to relax and enjoy the moment.

"We have time to walk a little farther. We'll gather firewood on our way back."

"Yeah." I gulp. I feel awkward. I've already thanked him. I don't want to talk about my job, the hospital or softball—at least not now. It's just the two of us in this isolated romantic setting. What do I say to an attractive and relatively new acquaintance?

"We need to turn around now and get to work on gathering some firewood."

"Yeah, sure." Damn it—I should have given him a signal.

"Good job, Kelly and Dan." Bev exclaims as we return to the campsite bearing armloads of firewood.

Two young Saudi men pull up in a car and wave to us and shout, "Hello."

Bob yells at them to go away. The two young men get out of the car and walk towards us. Bob puts his hands on his hips and walks towards them.

"Do you have matches?"

"Get out of here," Bob yells.

They do an about-face and drive away.

Bob says, "They are boys—too young to be driving. They want to look at Kelly and Bev because they don't have as many clothes on as their women do. There is simply no need for anybody to camp right next to us. They don't need matches."

"Bob, you know it's dangerous to get into a hassle," says Bev. "Bill Clark, a friend of ours, got into an altercation with a Saudi. Both were driving cars, they pulled up to a light, and the Saudi shook his fist at Bill. One thing led to another, and they wound up in a fist fight. Bill was deported. It is unwise to get into any fights with these people. Don't ever touch them. Even swearing or yelling at them could get you in deep trouble."

My heart sinks and my thoughts return to the incident in the Jeddah International Airport.

Bob faces Bev squarely, puts his hands on her shoulders, and thru clenched teeth, says, "No more Saudi talk."

I'm so glad Bob said that. I've got to refocus on the pleasures of this evening and suppress the memory of Tough Guy. And my swollen hand.

"For our first course," Bev demurely places her masterpiece of a classic Caesar salad before us.

"You've outdone yourself," Dan compliments Bev. She beams, but hints of stress around the corners of her mouth can't be concealed. With a white napkin wrapped around a jar, Dan pours white wine into our plastic cups.

"I'd like to propose a toast to Bev and her creation," I clear my throat and raise my plastic cup filled with homemade white wine. "I've had many, many Caesar salads but tonight this familiar arrangement looks more inviting than I can ever recall. The glistening, cool yellow-green broad blades of Romaine hearts confidently stretched across a platter in perfect harmony with the carefully scattered golden cubed croutons and shavings of innocent white cheese that lay lightly and leisurely on the blades. I'm pathetic, I know."

"No, you're not, Kelly," says Dan and kisses me on the cheek.

An easy discussion of favorite movies and recording artists supports our need to avoid argument or contentious debate.

The breeze off the sea wafts the delicious smell of steaks grilling on a fire. The mood is set for the banquet—mellow and not hurried.

In fresh plastic cups, Dan pours red wine for us. We bump our cups. The familiar trio of grill-marked steaks, big baked potatoes, and stalks of fresh buttered broccoli are served to us family style by Bob.

"It's just like home. Familiar is good. It's Bob's favorite meal," Bev says dreamily. Stories of favorite meals in favorite settings keeps us on our avoidance of conflict course. We are mellow and sated. The untouched round wooden bowl piled high with red apples, green pears, and purple grapes looks like a French impressionist painting that could be found on a wall at the Louvre. I wonder where the fresh fruit is imported from, but I don't ask. It really doesn't matter.

"Kelly, it's exactly 9:35. We've got all night, but I know you have curfew. You tell us when you want to leave." Bev stretches out on the blanket.

"Thanks, I will."

"Time for another stroll." Dan extends his hand and pulls me up from the blanket. This time, he puts his arm around my shoulder, and my arm goes comfortably around his waist. Under a trillion stars, we stroll in silence. This is so romantic I feel like I'm in another world. To comment on the magnificence of the moment would be vulgar. We stop. We face each other. My heart is pounding. If he doesn't kiss me, I will just have to kiss him. His hands are around my waist now. My hands are folded at the back of his neck. Gently and tenderly, his lips meet mine.

Affection and desire combine and combust.
Without dilemma, curfew is broken.

Chapter 10

Monday, September 21, 1987

Slugger and purse in hand, I burst out of 5350, and with speed, reach the main street. The minute I arrive at the hospital, I bump into Inger. She beams and says, "Softball tonight?"

"Right you are, Inger. I'll be there." I intend to keep walking so I can put Slugger in my office, before others see me with it. Inger tags along next to me.

"My superstar coach called me late last night. We couldn't get together because he's working on a special project for Mr. Zahran—the big guy from corporate."

"How nice." I don't correct the distortion. Inger chatters on and it seems Rick has led her to believe that once Mr. Zahran recognizes his talents and leadership abilities, he'll be rewarded with a promotion—maybe even replace King Khaled.

"So then Rick and I can go to Jeddah and get married."

"Married?"

"Yes, Kelly. It's easy. It's called a Saudi marriage around here. This license allows us to live together. When Rick's promoted we will move into an upscale Western married couples camp—take extravagant R&Rs every three months and live happily ever after."

"Really, Inger—is that realistic? What about work contracts and all that?" We arrive at my office and I tell her to come in and sit down. I stow the Slugger in the corner next to the filing cabinet.

"Well maybe it's not that easy," she says and she sits down. "But," she brightens, "if things don't work out you can just tear up the marriage license and go home."

"Well, I'll hope the best for you and Rick."

Inger leaves. I feel sad. Maybe I'm not a romantic or an optimist but just maybe I'm not as naïve as I thought I was. There is something weird about that fantastic scenario. I suspected yesterday that Rick's excitement over the pharmacy findings seemed opportunistic. I pray Inger doesn't get hurt.

Before I go to the conference room for the daily team meeting, I check in with Angelita. She greets me with a bright and sunny smile.

"What time is Mr. Zahran due to arrive?" Right after the question is out of my mouth, I wish that I hadn't asked it. She's got that amused look on her face that I've seen before. It's like she's got a secret or that she knows something that I don't know and maybe should know. I can't put my finger on it.

"Angelita, I need to plan my day—manage my time."

"Of course, you do. His plane has been delayed—we can expect him late morning or early afternoon."

"Thank you. Say, do you happen to know how Dr. Small's night went?"

"Just fine, Miss Day. He'll be released later today."

"That's great." I think Miss Day just hit a nerve.

Khaled and Rick are waiting for me when I enter the conference room. Khaled is not smiling but nods at me. Rick acknowledges me with a weak grin.

Khaled opens the meeting saying, "the authority has given their approval—all paperwork is in order. The hospital is providing two coolers filled with cans of soda, and an aluminum folding table—eight by three. A remote destination has been selected and it remains top secret. The drivers for the lead car and bus have been carefully chosen. They will leave a two-way radio with you and the girls in case of an emergency. They will go somewhere else and return at the appointed departure time. Miss Day, you will take the list of party-goers, reconcile the names on the list with the boarding passengers, and inquire if they have their Igamas with them. If not, you'll wait for them to retrieve them. Boarding will begin at 8:15 and departure is set for 8:30

sharp. The bus and the lead car will be waiting just inside the entrance of Camp Five."

Finally, he takes a breath.

"Mr. Al Kahairi, when will we be doing this?"

"Tomorrow morning."

"Tomorrow morning—I can't arrange work schedules on such short notice and I need to work on my sections of the report for Mr. Zahran ..."

Mr. Al Kahairi shifts in his chair, straightens his shoulders (I've seen this body language before—oh boy). He hesitates. I hold my breath.

"It must be done. The girls are unhappy."

I'm dumbfounded. "Okay. Consider it done."

King Khaled stands and leaves the conference room.

Rick smirks and says, "I think you'd better get on it, Miss Day."

"Oh be quiet, I will. But what's this about—some kind of an emergency—for God's sake?"

"I don't know, Kelly—maybe the element of surprise prevents planning any hanky-panky on the beach—you know how those parties can go." He smirks. "Or just maybe the King wants to impress on Wonder Boy that he's sensitive to the needs of the little nurses."

I laugh and say, "Rick, I have no idea what the beautiful and bright Inger could possibly see in you." He laughs too.

I go to my office, grab work schedules from the file cabinet, sit at my desk, unlock the top drawer, and pull out the secret list of those nurses who signed up for the beach party. I look at the postage stamp and think—it's a federal offense to divert narcotics, and just yesterday I was instrumental in likely uncovering such a deed. Today, I'm developing a plan to ensure a beach party is executed without incident. I must do this right—I don't want hanky-panky on my hands.

The big meeting is called. Angelita serves jasmine tea to Mr. Zahran and Mr. Al Kahairi. Mr. Jones, the pharmacy liaison from corporate, declines. I love the fragrance of jasmine so I accept the offer. Rick is content with a can of soda. Dr. Small is still a patient on the telemetry unit.

Rick leads off the meeting by suggesting irregularities in the procedure for accounting for every single narcotic. He mentions the abundance of antibiotics. He taps the file folder Dr. Small compiled on the pharmacy that's laying on the conference table. One would get the impression that these findings were uncovered by him. But when Mr. Jones starts asking questions, Rick lacks specifics. He reaches for a printout and takes a few minutes to review a page or two. Khaled and I watch Rick squirm.

Rick says, "The pharmacy is under Dr. Small's direction—Werner reports to him. Dr. Small is in the telemetry unit for observation, and he can explain this. It appears that he didn't have a heart attack."

I feel guilty taking just a little bit of pleasure in watching Rick sweat, and for some reason, I don't like that he's stepping on Khaled's toes. Rick looks at Mr. Al Kahairi and says, "Anything to add?"

Mr. Al Kahairi shrugs his shoulders. Rick turns to me. "Kelly—anything?"

"I think I can shed some light on this matter." I exchange chairs with Khaled to sit next to Mr. Jones. I pull notes from Dr. Small's file folder labeled pharmacy. I walk him through the findings and I explain to him exactly where in the pharmacy he can find enough antibiotics to treat a population ten times the size of this town.

Mr. Jones says, "Thank you. I'll take it from here." Mr. Zahran, Mr. Jones, and Khaled leave the room.

I look at Rick and say, "Let's check on Dr. Small." We arrive at Dr. Small's bedside in the telemetry unit. Angelita is there.

"Dr. Small expects to be given a clean bill of health and be discharged later today. When he's ready for discharge, I'll arrange for Moktar to drive him home," Angelita smiles. Dr. Small looks rested and content. Angelita seems so happy to be in charge of him.

At three in the afternoon, Mr. Zahran meets with Rick and me in Khaled's office. Khaled explains, "Mr. Jones will take over the pharmacy immediately and remain with us until a replacement can be found. Werner is on his way to jail. An investigation is underway."

Mr. Zahran politely thanks us for our good work and excuses himself as he has a plane to catch. I feel a little sad because Mr. Zahran and I made a nice connection when we first met, or at least I thought we did. But today it was as though we never met. He was so formal. I could kill Dr. Small for telling him I thought he was an attractive guy. Maybe he thinks I'm a decadent Western whore, who's after him.

At 3:00, Angelita and I help Dr. Small pack up his belongings. We walk him to the hospital exit where Moktar stands ready to drive him to his apartment. Angelita hands Dr. Small a neat package and says, "Just heat it up for twenty minutes at three-fifty. It's your favorite."

Before Moktar gets in the car, he motions to me. We meet near the trunk of the little white compact. He whispers to me, "Mr. Zahran asked me to tell you he would have liked to have spent some time with you before he left, but was afraid he'd miss his plane."

Moktar waits for my response. I hesitate. "Thanks for passing the message along." I know he wants more from me than that, but I hold back. For one thing, I'm not sure what I think about the message. I really would like to know what's on Zahran's mind.

I leave work with Slugger and make my way to camp Five. I've had a very busy day—I'm drained. If it weren't for Dan, I'd be tempted to miss the second softball game of my life. The memory of our romantic interlude last evening will remain with me for a long time—no matter how the story ends.

Somehow I get into 5350. I eat eight saltine crackers slathered with crunchy peanut butter, then another batch, and drink a diet Seven-Up. I forgot to eat lunch today. I change my clothes, grab Slugger by the neck and head for the Turf. I must hurry, I'm running late, I'm tired, and I miss Fidelis. It must be 90 degrees. I remind myself that Fidelis said softball is a healthy diversion—survival kit material.

.   .   .

At the Turf—I join my teammates—the Stoned Sands—I love that name. Most of them are housewives and I can't recall their names. Two are nurses from the hospital but my contact with them is fairly limited as they work in the operating room and start their day way earlier than me.

Dan greets us and organizes our fifteen minute warm-up. He calls all of us by our names. We'll play against the Smokin' Camels. We're scoreless after two innings. Something is going on, everyone seems distracted. Both games come to a halt.

There is commotion in the stands near the entrance to the Turf near our diamond—security jeeps and four security guys. Bob is walking towards the commotion. You can see some of the male spectators pulling out their Igamas and showing them to the security guys. I take a closer look and see that Zaynab is one of those spectators. As I recall, it was Bev who extended the invitation to him and his friend just recently, at the Big Bun.

A housewife says, "All of those guys surely don't have wives on our teams."   And the women start complaining that "nothing goes smoothly around here." I see Bev and Inger at a distance. I don't feel like joining them now—I fear guilt by association.

I'm determined as I stand here to keep my nose clean, so to speak. Dan is a temptation not only because he's a hot looking good guy, but this is a lonely place. There will be no romance for me in the Kingdom of Saudi Arabia.

Bob gathers all of us together and explains that, "Some single men were in the stands, but it's taken care of now. They've gone. Let's play ball."

I suspect Bob's downplaying the trouble. I tell myself to adjust my attitude and focus. It's my third at bat. I take a practice swing and adjust my grip. I check my stance, see the ball, swing, make contact. What a cool sound contact makes. Safe at first, I look around and have no idea where the ball is. I feel like a happy five-year old for the moment. But overall, the enthusiasm tonight compared to last week has declined—the final scores reflect less hits. Sands over Camels 3-2 and Royals over Bedouins 4-2.Dan congratulates us and highlights our best plays. He says, "see you all back here on Wednesday evening. Good night." Then he approaches me. "You really hit that ball hard. How did it feel?"

"Thanks." I shake my head and smile. "It really felt good."

"I'd offer you a ride but I already know the answer. And after tonight's little interruption, I understand your caution."

"Thank you for saying that, Dan. It helps me to know you understand. I've got to catch that bus." I head for the bus and notice out of the corner of my eye Bev and Bob are in a heated argument. No sign of Rick and Inger. I drop down to re-tie a loose shoe lace, get up just in time to see the white stretch limo leave. I'm in no shape to chase after it. I won't let that happen Wednesday evening. I'm out on the street all by myself. Thanks to Dan's coaching, I hit that ball well and it really did feel good. I can't help but wonder if his comment on caution can be interpreted as—"I won't be pursuing you anymore."

I stop at the entrance to Camp Five, take a deep breath, squeeze the Slugger. I wish I had a flashlight. My pace is slower now, I see a cat in the distance crossing the street. I turn at the bend in the maze that leads to Unit 5350. I hear the whine of a cat—like a baby's cry. I'm so miserable. I want to turn around and run out of the maze and to the hospital. I should have gone to the hospital and asked someone to walk me home. Next time.

I'm closer to 5350 and I notice the large trash can where I throw my garbage is even closer to my unit than it was this morning. The lid is ajar. How will I get past it? Cats and garbage cans go together. A security vehicle passes by. I feel like chasing after it. Would they help me? I wait, think, finally decide to run past the trash can—one, two, three—go. I'm so near it—Oh, God. Three cats jump out of the can and the lid crashes to the pavement. A cat scampers over my foot; I swing the bat low to the ground, in order to shoo them away, as more cats jump out of the can—I accidentally hit the can and it tips over.

I'm shaking like a leaf and the security vehicle pulls up and a uni-formed man gets out. I stand frozen in place with Slugger in hand.

. . .

I am behind bars—locked in a cage and I don't know why. When I entered this cinder-block, austere one-story building, I assumed I would be questioned by a police officer, answer their questions, and explain my situation. A simple story: hospital nurse goes to play a game of women's softball and simply forgets to put her Igama in her pocket. But no—no one talks to me. Possibly they're waiting for an interpreter to arrive. I shouldn't be locked up. I am really afraid. I'd like to scream, kick, and try to fight my way out of here. But I choose to cooperate hoping that calmness and politeness will gain me some-thing. I can't allow my fears to cause me to do something I'll regret. The event in the Jeddah airport will burn in my memory forever.

I think I'm the only English speaking person here. I've counted only three uniformed men moving about—I've seen no women. Worst of all for me, a black cat sits on the desk of the guard who's watching me from a distance of less than fifteen feet. I couldn't be more miserable. My jailer has absolutely no idea how terrified and trapped I feel.

I'm so distraught I can't even cry. I'm not a criminal. I can't sleep on the little cot. I'll just sit here, feel sorry for myself and monitor the cat's behavior. I doubt that it would jump off the desk, creep in to my cell, and scratch me to death. I know that rationally, but—it happens in movies, in nightmares, and in the minds of people who have cat phobia. My worst nightmare—cornered by a big black cat. My luck is unbelievably bad.

I've never stolen as much as a thumb-tack, never told a lie of any consequence. I smoked a cigarette behind the garage at the age of thir-teen with Larry, the boy two-doors down the street. I skipped one day of school near the end of my senior year, and sassed my parents prob-ably no more than ten times during my adolescence.

I reason that by virtue of my living in Camp Five they must know that I work at the hospital. Two security guys were just at my apartment last night—the broken pipe—Peeping-Tom incident. Why don't they call Mr. Al Kahairi—employer? What do they call them again—sponsors? My only consolation is that I will be missed at the hospital in the morning. Then this can all be cleared up. If my jailers only knew that I have an important secret mission to complete tomorrow morning. If I could just explain things.

The last time I was awake all night was in the Jeddah International Airport. That uncomfortable night is no match for this agonizing night locked behind bars, held prisoner more by a black cat than steel bars and an old jailer. I must focus on my release in the morning and not let my mind wander to dark places. I will not panic.

The black cat and jailer are sleeping now. The jailer alternates between loud snorts, quiet breathing, and periods of no breathing at all. He's obese and I'll bet a heavy smoker. I diagnose him with a condition called sleep apnea. It's not a good thing when your breathing stops at intervals during sleep. The black cat, however, all stretched out, sleeps peacefully. I can't believe my situation. In a million years I could never have imagined a night like this.

Chapter 11

Tuesday, September 22, 1987

It's 6:00 a.m. and two women completely covered in black, faces covered by veils, not even the eyes exposed, stand by as the jailer unlocks the cell door and I'm motioned to follow the women. I'm offered the opportunity to use a toilet and a sink in private and I take advantage of the opportunity.

I'm returned not to the cell but a table. I'm given a cup of water, a cup of coffee and what looks like a scrambled egg over rice, a fork and a small paper napkin. The women leave me at the table. The coffee is hot. The eggs taste funny. I have three forkfuls of rice.

I hear several male voices speaking in Arabic from a distance. The voices get louder, I swallow hard and now this entourage is standing about ten feet in front of me—Mr. Al Kahairi, Moktar, two uniformed men and Angelita. I am not acknowledged. I remain seated. Angelita looks scared, makes eye contact with me, then looks down at the floor.

Mr. Al Kahairi raises his voice, a uniformed man raises his. Moktar takes over in what it seems to be an attempt to arbitrate. The debate or argument picks back up then slowly simmers down. Moktar is clearly in control—if body language and tone of voice mean anything. A uniformed man leaves and returns with, of all things, my Louisville Slugger. He hands it to Moktar. Within minutes I am walking out of the jail house with three friends and Slugger. Angelita and I get in the back seat of the little white compact. Moktar is behind the wheel and Mr. Al Kahairi is twisted sideways in the passenger seat attempting to face me and Angelita.

"Miss Day, the police thought that you were trying to beat the cats to death with that bat you carry around with you—very suspicious. I had to explain your suspicious behavior. Believe me, it wasn't easy.

You didn't have your Igama with you—also very suspicious. I told you about that." He sighs—a martyr's sigh.

"Mr. Al Kahairi, I am truly, truly sorry for the inconvenience I have caused you. The Igama is in my unit. I forgot to take it to the softball game. I am so sorry."

Moktar pulls up the car as close as he can to 5350. I put my hand on the car door handle and Khaled says, "Miss Day, the beach trip will take place as planned. Enjoy yourself."

"Thank you, Mr. Al Kahairi. I won't forget your help with this unfortunate incident."

All I can think of is our first and second meetings—I can see him patting the telephone on his desk and saying, "When anything happens—I get the call." I guess he got the call. Little did I know then, or could in my wildest dreams imagine, he'd get "the call" about me.

. . .

It's 8:15. I sling a large tote bag over my shoulder which contains the manila envelope with the list of partygoers, a jar of nuts, and a bag of potato chips. I planned on making a large batch of deviled eggs (something I can do well) last evening after the game, but my good intentions were thwarted by a colossal misunderstanding, not to mention my careless behavior: leaving 5350 without my local passport.

I join the growing number of nurses assembling at the entrance of Camp Five in anticipation of a trip to the seashore. The lead car pulls in and parks, followed by the white stretch limo. The driver of the lead car steps out and I do a double take. My jaw drops. I look away. I look back.

"Moktar?" I ask, "Is that you?" All heads turn towards him and a wave of giggles shimmer over the crowd. Unabashedly, he grins. He is without headdress, wearing a short sleeved white T-shirt and short white shorts. He looks downright naked. He must have friends in high places to have the temerity to show up so scantily clothed. Watching him get out of the small white compact was funnier than twenty-five clowns stepping out of a Volkswagen at a circus.

The bus driver is Jo Jo, a Filipino guy who works in maintenance and is familiar to all of us. I pull out the list of names, and do a roll call. The bus leaves at 8:30 promptly.

Laughter abounds, and picture taking gets underway. Just about everyone has a camera. Our party numbers thirty-three: I am the only Westerner, among thirty Filipinos and two Muslim women. There is Poey, our pediatric head nurse from Thailand, and Asima, the wife of one of our physicians. Asima and her husband are Palestinians with Jordanian passports.

Merrily we roll along on paved roads where we see an occasional gas station and some abandoned cars here and there. When we transition to dirt roads, the gas stations disappear and abandoned cars are replaced by a camel here and there.

Jo Jo brings the bus to a halt. Violeta, the exuberant young nurse, who entertained us with several songs at Michelle's birthday party, takes charge. She shouts to Jo Jo, "that beach looks dirty. Drive on."

Jo Jo leaves the bus, confers with Moktar, returns, and starts up the bus. The nurses are on their feet and cheering. Within minutes we stop again. We wait for Violeta to render an opinion. With formality and fanfare, she gives Jo Jo two thumbs up, and the nurses cheer again. Violeta, our hero, now takes the lead and organizes the picnic: Beach blankets here, coolers over there, beach umbrellas there, there, and there. She directs Jo Jo to re-park the bus to provide more shade for the picnic table. The bus becomes the changing room. Colorful bikinis and shorts and T-shirts parade from the steps of the bus and down a lumpy and sandy runway to the beach. The exception: Poey and Asima who are dressed modestly in cotton long pants and long-sleeved blouses and scarves about their hair, faces showing.

Moktar takes our collective breath away for a second time. Shirtless and shoeless, he mingles among us. I am dumbfounded. This can't be the man who picked me up at the airport less than two weeks ago. Jo Jo mingles as well but in a t-shirt and trunks.

There is swimming and wading, clicking of cameras, bouncing beach balls, sunbathing and music blaring from a battery powered tape deck. We are having fun, pure and simple.

Violeta shouts, "come and get it!" But first, with sweet deference to our wonderful drivers, they are each presented a plate heaped with eggrolls, a chicken concoction, fried rice, green salad, and a dessert called leche. Jo Jo and Moktar beam. Then the women line up at the smorgasbord and help themselves.

With my overloaded plate in hand, I make my way to a large blanket stretched out in the shade of the white stretch limo, and join Violeta, Jo Jo, and Moktar. Violeta is explaining her recipe for chicken adobo, which is the featured dish on all of our plates. Moktar takes to teasing her about little Filipino nurses who eat every two hours and never gain weight. She giggles and says, "we love to eat!"

Jo Jo says, "wait until you get to the leche. It's very rich and melts in your mouth."

I ask about the leche and learn it's made up of evaporated milk, sugar, and eggs.

Jo Jo and Violeta laugh as Moktar is attempting to pronounce "siopao," a Tagalog word for a white ball of dough with a hard-boiled egg and chicken inside it. It gets even funnier when he attepts "cassava bibingka." Best I can gather, it's some kind of a pudding/rice cake.

Violeta checks her wristwatch and says it's time to get ready to leave. Moktar and I insist that we dispose of Violeta and Jo Jo's plates and cups. While alone, Moktar says, "Angelita will be able to tell you about Fidelis." He looks sad and his non-verbal communication tells me not to pursue this with him.

Violeta orchestrates the plan to return to Camp Five. Because some of the nurses will work the afternoon shift and some will need to rest prior to working the midnight shift, she sets the departure time for 2:15. We all pitch in and pack up, bagging garbage and folding blankets.

The ride back to Camp Five is subdued. Some are napping, others are talking quietly. There is a peacefulness tinged with sorrow. I wonder about Fidelis. I miss her. I reflect on today's event and how it came to be. Triggered by a rumor about a wall and the threat of mass resignations, this lovely interlude was born. It's significant that the wall was never mentioned. We departed from the strict game plan, and savored the sweet defiant act of allowing our drivers to embed themselves in our all-girl beach party. I firmly believe our unspoken and smug collective act of defiance will never reach the ears of Mr. Khaled Al Kahairi, or the Authority, or Corporate.

I ask Violeta to walk me to 5350. I don't need to lie about an allergy or confess about a phobia. The world knows. She enters the gate first and returns quickly. She has deep furrows between her eyebrows that I've never seen before. She looks like she's forty, unhappy, not anything like the twenty-something, singer, dancer, mistress of ceremonies at birthday parties and beach soirees.

"What?" My heart sinks.

"Kelly, do you have trash bags in your apartment?"

"Yeah—what's wrong, Violeta?"

"Give me your keys, I'm going to clean your doorstep and then we'll talk about it."

"Are you sure?"

"Yes."

I hand her the keys. "The supplies are under the kitchen sink."

I stand in the sun in the street outside 5350. I can't imagine what's on my doorstep. I'll know soon enough. I am indebted to so many folks here. Fidelis, Violeta for this kind deed, Dan for the snorkeling adventure and my base hit, Bev and Bob, and Moktar and Mr. Al Kahairi, and even Jan and Carolyn for trying to clue me in on things— even if they have a strange way of going about it. I don't feel like thirty —I feel like forty.

Violeta swings open the gate with a bag in hand and marches to the garbage can, removes the lid, tosses bag, puts lid back on securely. She pushes the gate open and turns to me and waves me into the court-yard. We sit at the table and drink Diet Seven-Up. Sadly, I learn that a very dead cat—days dead—was placed on my doorstep. I have an enemy.

I phone the hospital and ask for Mr. Al Kahairi. I report to him that the beach party was a success. We're all back safe and sound. I ask him to transfer me to Angelita. I invite her to dinner. I tell her I have some wonderful adobo chicken left over from the beach party. Invitation accepted. I set my alarm for 6:00 p.m. and take a nap.

. . .

I'm fixing a salad when the doorbell rings. Angelita is dressed casually in blue jeans and a colorful floral print blouse. She joins me in the kitchen and advises on the oven temperature and length of time the chicken adobo should be heated up. I give her the highlights of the beach party. We agree that the world is a better place because of Violeta. She asks about the women's softball team and how it's going. I summarize. I'm getting the decided impression that she doesn't socialize very much.

I clear the table and serve us coffee. I think we've exhausted superficial chit-chat. So, I take a deep breath, choosing my words carefully, "I'm very fond of Fidelis. Can you tell me anything about her sudden departure?"

"Somebody had to accompany Carmencita back home."

"I know that, Angelita. But, it's usually a nurse, right?"

Angelita adverts her eyes and says, "Yes, but ... "

"I'll tell you, Angelita, I felt very close to Fidelis and I don't believe she would have left without saying a word to me."

"Alright, Kelly, I'll start at the beginning. Fidelis had an affair with a Filipino man who worked at the company that is subcontracted to manage housing units in all the camps—upkeep and repairs—that sort of thing. His contract expired and he returned to the Philippines about six months ago. Shortly after that, she found out thru contacts in Manila that he was married with children and that he was very ill. She became depressed and her weight started to drop.

"Can you keep a secret?"

"Yes, I can."

"Dr. Small noticed her weight loss and depression just recently—just before you arrived, actually. He talked with her and put her on an anti-depressant. But he wasn't satisfied. He wanted to run some tests. Fidelis wouldn't have any part of it—at first. On Thursday she came to see Dr. Small in his office. The three of us met. She consented to a blood test."

"She told me that morning that the tryouts wore her out—she looked bad."

"We wanted no record of the blood draw or the results, so we waited until evening. Dr. Small drew Fidelis's blood himself right in his office. It was early evening and the hospital was relatively quiet. He had difficulty finding a good vein, and he contaminated the needles, so I had to go to the lab to get extra needles and tubes. That wasn't easy. I have no business in the lab, so I pretended I was delivering memos that I had already circulated the week before. I took the needles and tubes when the technician, Sunil's, back was turned, all the while worrying about getting my hand chopped off. Everything we did was on the sly because we wanted no record of this. If Sunil saw something suspicious, he would have reported it to somebody for sure. He's so grateful for his job here that he works very hard to please Mr. Al Kahairi."

"I can imagine."

"After several attempts and blood everywhere, Homer got the sample. All the while, Fidelis was quiet and patient. Then we sent her home to rest and we waited for the call to prayer.

When the call to prayer was proclaimed from the minarets, I went to the lobby to watch for Sunil to head for the mosque. I used the phone in the lobby to call Homer. I say, 'all clear.' Dr. Small headed for the lab with the blood sample hidden in his lab coat pocket. He ran the sample thru the autoanalyzer and waited for the results. But Sunil had re-entered the hospital, so I paged Dr. Small overhead immediately to alert him of Sunil's return. That was to serve as the signal and it did. We met back in his office. The blood analysis had been completed. He had turned the autoanalyzer off, but he didn't have time to hit the button on the printer to get the results."

"I'm impressed with your plan."

"But, Kelly, we had to revise our plan. We decided to call Sunil and ask him to come to Dr. Small's office. He agreed, then Dr. Small hid in the hallway. When Sunil entered his office, I gave him a cup of tea and asked him to wait here for Dr. Small. By that time Dr. Small was on his way to the lab to print out the result. I engaged Sunil in conversation as long as I could. I asked him about the Sinhalese people, the Tamil Tigers, and how he got here. I actually knew his story as almost every employee knows his story well. He's lonely, well-liked, and known for telling his story to anyone who will listen."

"That was a good idea."

"Well, it all had been working until … Sunil commented on the blood on the arm of the chair that he was sitting in and on the floor near his feet. I explained to him that Dr. Small's ear bleeds frequently and it's probably his blood. Sunil looked very skeptical. I'm not the best liar."

"God, Angelita—that was good thinking. Sunil may be known for telling his personal account of a civil war in his homeland, seeking refuge here and all that—but Dr. Small's bloody ear is, bar none, the mostly publically talked about phenomenon here at the hospital."

"True, Kelly. Well, then I excused myself—called Homer in the lab and told him to be sure his ear is bleeding when he returns to the office. He did as instructed. Blood was on his ear, his neck, and lapel, and the printout of lab results was stuffed in his back pocket. He was so nervous that he chatted with Sunil for forty-five minutes and concluded with, 'I just wanted to get to know you better, thanks for stopping by.

"The next morning, Friday, Dr. Small met with me and Fidelis. He was wonderful, so sensitive. He reviewed the results of the blood test with us. Our worst fears were confirmed—Fidelis had a dangerously low white cell count. You know what that means."

I nod my head and say, "Ability to fight infections is compromised —there could be many reasons for this, Angelita, and maybe an easy explanation and solution."

"Anyway, based on the blood results, weight loss and fatigue, we moved up Carmencita's departure date and put Fidelis in the role of escort. It was almost impossible to make any arrangement on Friday, but, we—as they say—'got a little help from a friend.' Saturday was touch and go but we got it done."

"How's she doing? What's being done?"

"She's having tests done in Manila. She asked me to tell you her story and apologize for not sharing anything with you. She knows that you care about her."

"I sure do. I wish I could do something. Can I write to her?"

"Kelly, all this is very confidential. So, no, you can't write just now. I will update you as soon as I can."

"Angelita, I have some money I could send …"

"Not now, Kelly—but thanks."

We hug goodnight.

I think about Angelita. She is a sweet young lady who really doesn't talk about herself, often appears amused, and is generally happy. I do know that she tells a good story and she's very fond of Homer. I got the impression tonight that she doesn't socialize much. She wasn't at the big birthday bash—didn't join the women's softball league and I remember asking her to come to the beach party, but she declined. She's got a secret—Dr. Small? Can't be—he's likely oblivious to her crush on him—with the ear thing, wishing his wife were here, overall anxiety—he's probably clueless. Right now it's easier for me to specu-late on the life of mysterious Angelita, than begin to speculate on the underlying cause of Fidelis's low white cell count. I will not jump to any conclusions. It could be something simple and easily corrected.

My night is long, fitful, and mostly sleepless.

Chapter 12

Wednesday, September 23, 1987

Somehow, without Slugger, my outlaw companion, now retired, I get out of 5350 and drag myself to the hospital. My morning starts with a bang.

"Steve, what's going on?"

He shouts, "Here, look at this bloody rubbish!" He punches the front page of the Saudi Gazette, shaking his head in disgust.

I scan the article, basically, it says: by royal decree an income tax on foreigners will be imposed, effective January 20th, 1988. It goes on to give the numbers for individuals and corporations.

I caution Steve, red faced and perspiring, to cool down before he has a heart attack or gets fined for loud and disruptive behavior. I go to other areas and it's the same scene. Copies of the Saudi Gazette are all over the nurses' stations and the chatter is negative. Everything from, "I'm quitting," to an anguished, "how will I tell this to my family." No one is holding back—the anger is palpable. It makes me edgy.

The administrative meeting is moved up to eight o'clock. Khaled takes the lead. He has a copy of the Saudi Gazette in front of him. "The royal decree about taxing the income of expats is something we cannot address. That's the way it is. Inshalla."

"It screws up everything. Poor morale, resignations, it could be a disaster," Rick complains.

"Patients may not get the best care. Maybe no care … we're the only show in town," says Dr. Small.

"At best we can remind the staff that it will not go into effect until late January," I say.

Rick says, "we've all got reports to write—our work is important." He refines the work plan, breaking it down into small pieces. He has a knack for explaining things in ways that make it seem as though he believes that you know what you're doing, and he's just clarifying to make sure we're all on the same page. He emphasizes the importance of looking carefully at workloads, staffing, scheduling, inventory, budgets, and policies and procedures.

He says, "The more we dig, the more questions we'll have—and that's a good thing. If we find something that we don't understand, or if we think a problem exists, it's likely we've hit upon an area ripe for improvement. This is what we want—an opportunity to improve what we do and how we do it. I can't stress enough the importance of interviewing your staff to gain an understanding of how the department really works, what their issues are—complaints—all of it."

Just when I'm convinced he's an idiot, besides a male chauvinistic pig already, he impresses me. Dr. Small looks completely lost, complains of gastritis, wishes his wife were here, and reminds us again that he doesn't have an MBA degree. No one asks me about yesterday's nurse's day at the beach, or about my jail time.

"One last thing. I recommend that we use a report-writing format that I developed while in grad school. I aced all the business writing courses and my peers paid me to write their reports." Rick passes to each of us the format and an attached sample report. Dr. Small looks at me and winks. Khaled's eyes narrow.

"Let's meet at the end of the day—4:00 okay?" says Rick.

We nod in agreement.

I decide to visit my areas of responsibility again and listen to the staff mutter about the royal decree. The wall has been forgotten about. Anger, disgust, sadness, and disbelief consume the staff. The Saudi patients and visitors are noticeably quiet and less demanding. Carolyn and Jan tell me that they'll leave at the end of January and live together either in the UK or US. Steve says he doesn't know where to go next but he is still planning a swell party before this all ends, and my invitation stands. Inger is still talking about marrying Rick. Poey looks sad and lost.

I sit at my desk and stare at the postage stamp and wonder how my elderly parents are doing back home in that wealthy, democratic nation. They will never know that the little bundle they plucked from an orphanage in Dublin, Ireland, over thirty years ago, spent last night in a jail cell in Yanbu, Saudi Arabia.

Dr. Small knocks on my door and comes in and sits down. "I don't know what I'll do. My wife is not here yet. I'll probably resign, I think. I tried to call her when I saw the headlines in the Gazette this morning. With the time change and all, I get mixed up. She probably was sleeping. I'll try later maybe. I don't know. How are your reports coming along?"

I get up and hand him a tissue for his ear. "To Rick's credit, he has coached us well—the format and sample are worthy of publication in a business journal."

Dr. Small laughs and says, "I just assumed he lifted it from a journal."

I laugh. "You might be right about that."

"What are the consequences for breaking a contract?"

"It's costly, Kelly—very costly. Supposedly, if you break your contract two months' notice is required and the forfeiture of one month's salary, as well as paying your own way home." He stops talking. He gets up and says, "I'm going to try and call my Constantia."

"How about if I bring you some pizza from the Palace? Everything on it?"

He smiles, "Yes, yes. Let me give you some riyals." He struggles to locate his wallet.

"My treat, Homer. See you later."

. . .

Sitting alone in the family section of the Pizza Palace, I review my options and wait for my order. Resignation effective as soon as I can get a flight out? I imagine getting a flight out could be difficult if everyone who threatens to leave actually does. I could go out on R&R and abandon my contract like I heard so many do. If I abandon my contract or resign, I won't be partying in Bangkok or London. I'll have to pay U.S. income tax on the money I've earned here. I need to complete one full year of work outside the U.S. to realize the benefits of U.S. income tax exemption. I chew on a slice. No job waiting for me in Ohio. No pot of gold tucked under my arm when I exit the Kingdom.

. . .

I deliver a large Pepsi and a medium pizza with everything on it to Dr. Small's office. He's on the phone. I go to my office. I'm unmotivated to write anything or do anything. I don't think today is a good day to interview staff.

I feel the need to visit my areas again, check their pulse again, so to speak, before I immerse myself in data. This time, I find Steve munching on a jelly donut and sipping coffee—content as can be. He is an enigma to me. Jan and a doctor are setting a simple fractured humerus bone of a seven year old Saudi girl. The girl is the third victim of the second car accident we've treated this morning. I'm reminded that I doubted almost everything Carolyn told me upon my arrival, and now it seems every day something happens that substantiates at least some of her claims. Inger is inserting a needle in the arm of a young Saudi male so he can receive intravenous fluids while a surgeon explores an enormous gash on the back of his skull. Carolyn is busy delivering a set of twins. Moktar sits at a desk talking on the phone in Arabic. He's calling patients to remind them of their clinic appointments. I seriously doubt that Moktar is a one-man mafia. But then … It's good everyone is back to work. I need to refocus as well.

. . .

Back at my desk again, my mind wanders to Mr. Zahran. I wonder what he'd think of a woman with a neurotic fear of cats, getting herself locked up in jail. I wonder about his message that Moktar mentioned —wishing that he had more time to spend with me. That reminds me

—he asked me about disaster preparedness. He probably just wanted to talk business.

I pull the Disaster Manual off the shelf. Study it—line by line— make notes to myself and a list of questions. I was on the hospital disaster committee back home and helped prepare and execute the annual mock disaster drills a number of times. This plan, in my opinion, is well written and thorough.

Rick touches base with me minutes before our meeting with the team. He says he wants me to play "dumb blonde" and ask a lot of questions. That way Khaled and Dr. Small won't have to ask them thereby saving face. I admit to Rick his strategy is wise and I thank him for saying play dumb blonde.

We meet as planned. Khaled starts off, "Mr. Zahran would like a preliminary report as soon as possible."

"That's dandy—we'll just push a little harder," says Rick.

.   .   .

Without Fidelis or Slugger I trudge to the Saudi Turf alone. Slugger is officially retired. I join a few of my teammates whom I only know by sight—I'm determined to learn their names this evening. I see Dan —I smile and wave. Next thing I know, Bob is calling all of us to gather around for a few announcements.

"Hi, everybody—glad to see you. We've had to make some adjustments—a few players have dropped out. So we've eliminated the Bedouins—sorry about that."

"What'd he say?" Mumbles and groans ripple through our little crowd.

"I apologize. But, I think we've balanced the remaining three teams very well." He reads out the new team assignments. I've been removed from the Stoned Sands and assigned to the Smokin' Camels. I've got new teammates and to my disappointment—a new coach—named Greg.

Bob drops the next bomb. "After each team warms up for fifteen minutes, we'll start off with our first game. The Royal Oils versus

Stoned Sands. They'll play five innings. In the meantime, Greg will hold practice with the Smokin' Camels. We'll take a break after the first game—for fifteen minutes. Then the Smokin' Camels will play the winning team from the first game."

Again, there's muttering and groaning. Bob pitches his voice above the crowd and says, "ladies it's all about good sportsmanship, athleticism, recreation, diversion, fun, and play."

Then he shouts out the letters—as though our lives depended on it —"H-A-V-E F-U-N P-L-A-Y B-A-L-L!" It's like when parents spell out words so the children don't know what is being said. We're all laughing very hard now.

I'm trying to memorize the names of my Smokin' Camel teammates, while focusing on throwing and catching, and at the same time wondering if the commotion during Monday night's game was the cause of the drop outs, or if it was the royal decree on income tax. I miss Slugger as I practice batting. My arm is getting sore as I practice throwing. I can't wait for the fifteen minute break.

The Royal Oils easily triumph 6-1 over my former team the Stoned Sands. Rick is beating his chest and Inger is swooning. Dan finds me. We're both laughing and neither of us has said a word yet.

"Where's your bat?"

"Dan, believe me—I can't explain it right now—it's an unbelievable story."

He shakes his head, "Nothing is unbelievable here."

We smile at each other.

"Give it your best, Kelly."

"I will."

Bases loaded. I smack the ball with a force I didn't know I had. One run in—bases loaded again—two outs. Damn! Pop out—inning over. Camels and Oils tied 4-4 end of the fourth.

Now what? There's a commotion again—security is here. The commotion this time is behind home plate. I'm looking around and trying to figure things out—it's mayhem. All my team mates as well as the other players are moving towards home plate. That doesn't seem like a good idea to me—I'm not going to follow the crowd—my dad, a retired cop, schooled me to think for myself when a crowd gets fired up. I turn around and head for the street as fast as I can. I've got my Igama and my keys to 5350 in my pocket. My adrenaline is flowing—this is the fastest I've ever moved in my life.

For the first time in my life the feline phobia takes a back seat to another fear. I stamp my feet in front of the gate, unlatch it, dart for the door of 5350, key it, and slam it behind me. Safe for now.

After a shower, I dial Dan's number—no answer. Bev and Bob—no answer. Inger—no answer. I make a plan to dial these numbers again in the same order every fifteen minutes until someone picks up. In my magical thinking, I believe that if I execute this procedure with precision, remain resolute and persevere, someone will eventually respond to the ringing.

After the seventh round of dial-ups, I grab a one-pound bag of frozen kernel corn from the refrigerator. In a sauce pan on the stove top I boil the hell out of the kernels, drain them, throw careless amounts of butter, salt, and pepper on them. Using an old metal fork with two of the four tines damaged, I shovel the kernels into my mouth forkful after forkful—all the while big, fat, salty tears spill over the lower lids of my eyeballs, slide down my cheeks and splash onto already over-salted kernels.

I restart the procedure at the fifteen minute mark. I'm losing steam and I'm having a hard time staying awake. It's 2:00 a.m. when I reluctantly concede that there's no magic to my formula—no human voice on the other end—no psychic comfort obtained.

Chapter 13

Thursday, September 24, 1987

Damnit! I've overslept. I race to the hospital in the heat—swear under my breath at the cats. I hate them. It's their fault I went to jail.

I go straight to the conference room. "Sorry I'm late."

"Good morning, Miss Kelly. It's the wonderful half-day Thursday," says Rick without making eye contact.

Dr. Small looks rested, and there's no blood on his ear.

Mr. Al Kahairi squares his shoulders. "Good morning. Just some history. Eight months ago I was appointed by the Royal Commission to assume the leadership of this hospital. I was honored. Six months ago Dr. Small arrived. Mr. Savage—two months ago. Miss Day," he tips his head in my direction, "joined us, what is it now? Almost two weeks ago." He smiles broadly. Clears his throat. "I'll be in town this weekend—meaning Thursday afternoon and Friday, if you should happen to be working on your reports," he chuckles, "in your spare time, if you have any questions about our customs or anything at all that may or may not affect hospital operations, call me as I am an available resource. I'm just a phone call away. Take my phone number down now."

He stands, walks a few steps, turns towards the three of us. Mounts his big hands—fingers entwined on his big belly and sounding like a disapproving high school teacher doling out a homework assignment, he enunciates clearly and distinctly, "402 03 77." You can hear graphite stroking paper. Without another word, he leaves.

The three of us look at each other. Of course, Dr. Small speaks first. "What was that about? I mean he was different—I think." He gets up and says, "I'll see you two later—I'd better do some interviews so I know what the hell I'm talking about in my radiology report."

"Rick, we need to talk—let's go to my office."

"I'll grab a cup of coffee and be right with you—want some?"

"No thanks, my stomach is killing me."

"Do you want a soda—tea?"

"No, really, Rick, thanks." I sit at my desk and stare at the postage stamp. I stew about Khalid's remarks this morning and focus on "any questions about our customs." His demeanor was supercilious. We're on his turf and he's in charge—even if Rick and I have more knowledge and experience with hospital operations than him. I owe Khaled for rescuing me from jail or is it Moktar that I owe? Nonetheless, I'm grateful to both. I'm out of jail.

Rick closes the door. We sit at the little round table. He takes a gulp of coffee. "This is the way it is, Kelly. Dan's in jail. Security went to his place last evening while he—we were at the Turf. They found wine in his apartment. Well, actually, a kit to make wine beside a supply of wine. If they think he sells it—that makes matters worse for him. The bastards could have him by the ..."

"Can they just break in like that?" My heart sinks.

"They say it's their property—we're just using it—and they often make some bullshit of an excuse—like checking broken water pipes—anything."

"That sounds familiar. What's going to happen to him? What about his sponsor?"

"We don't know yet. Bob is going to try to pull some strings. They're just friends—Dan works for a smaller company—but Bob will try to use his clout."

"I called Dan, Bev and Bob, and Inger numerous times last night—no answer."

"Inger and I scrambled last night while the focus was obviously on Dan. Remember I'm still house-sitting."

"I forgot you were. But why, Dan?"

"We think Dan was the target."

"Why?" I hear myself screech.

"No idea, Kelly. Single and coaching women's softball—suspected of peddling homemade wine? Who knows. I know you like him. He is a good guy. As soon as I know something—I'm in touch with Bob—you'll know something."

"Why did Khaled act the way he did this morning—so ...?""Kelly, I'm sure he knows about the raid at the Turf last evening. He knows I fool around. He's putting me on notice—I'm guessing. I plan to write the best report I can—make him look good—not me. He intimidated the hell out of me this morning—after Dan's arrest and all."

"Rick, Khaled and Moktar fished me out of jail. I'm in his debt—big time."

"Kelly, you, me, and Inger—we're not behind bars today. Look, I'm going to run some errands. I'll pick up sandwiches for us and Dr. Small too. What difference does it make if we have the afternoon off. We might as well get our shit together."

"I couldn't agree with you more. The team of Small, Savage, and Day will knock out an extraordinary report."

"We can do this, Kelly. Oh, I forgot, the Women's Softball League is temporarily suspended."

I laugh. "No kidding. Fidelis used to say softball is survival kit material—as far as I'm concerned Russian roulette would be safer."

Rick leaves and I stare at the postage stamp once again. Politics makes strange bedfellows.

. .

Dr. Small asks Angelita to work with us which is a really good idea. The typing is a big job and because of Angelita's role as executive administrative secretary, she's a veritable treasure house of information. It's fun to see her smile and give us that look when she snaps answers to our questions, or directs us where to find answers. She's having a ball and it's great having her with us. At least one of us is cheerful.

I share with the team the question Mr. Zahran asked about disaster preparedness and my analysis of the hospital's plan.

Rick gets excited and runs on about water desalination plants, the major sea port, local oil refineries, the price of oil, the transition from Aramco running the show to the Saudis, and Saudi concerns about sabotage from outside and inside the Kingdom. He's off and running with disaster scenarios. Rick has a great imagination and could win a prize for concocting sinister plots. He retells the episode of the TV soap Dallas where J. R. Ewing pays big bucks to a psychopathic mercenary who's eager to blow up a few Saudi oil fields. Dr. Small reminisces about the episode with him. I'm bored with their nonsense.

We're finally off that subject and back on track. The team agrees that whoever laid the foundation for this little hospital five years ago knew what they were doing. We're feeling good as a team.

"We've dotted our i's and crossed our t's. This is as good as it gets," says Rick.

"I have nothing to do tomorrow. I think we should meet here again. We could make slides—transparencies—use an overhead projector—it could be really cool."

Rick looks at me and says, "I'm sorry you don't have anything to do tomorrow."

Dr. Small says, "I'm exhausted. I'm going to get caught up on my sleep tomorrow."

Angelita says, "Kelly, we don't have the equipment—sorry."

Something tells me that Rick and Inger will spend the day together at the married couple's love nest and just maybe Angelita will be cooking up something nice for poor Dr. Small, whose wife just can't seem to find that marriage certificate. I feel like a jealous old maid.

It is 8:30 p.m. and we're ready to call it a night. Surprise, Khaled enters the conference room. All I can think is, thank God we weren't having fun at his expense.

He flashes a broad smile and says, "I've been calling you at your apartments. I have two announcements to make." He remains standing—big hands mounted on big belly.

Rick kicks my foot under the table.

Homer says, "It's nice to see you—what a surprise," as his fingers go to the ear.

Angelita and I keep quiet. I hold my breath. Angelita quietly slinks into a chair.

"The royal decree has been rescinded. It'll be in all the papers on Saturday." He beams.

"Great, great, super," says Dr. Small.

"The staff will be delighted," I add. Rick kicks me again. "And for news of another matter." You could hear a pin drop. Mr. Al Kahairi announces, "Mr. Zahran will be here Saturday—10:30 a.m. Inshallah."

Rick speaks up and says, "we're ready for him. Let me give you your copy of the final draft. Look it over. We'd be happy for your input, any suggestions, comments …"

"Fine. I'll review it. In the meantime, I want you to enjoy your day off tomorrow. Do something fun. All work and no play makes for a dull Johnny—isn't that what they say?" Mr. Al Kahairi turns and leaves.

"If I didn't know better I'd think he was stoned," Rick says.

Oh, God, he's returned to the conference room.

"I heard that, Mr. Savage. Believe me, I'm not stoned as you say."

I can't look anywhere but down. If the tension in this room could be measured on a Richter scale, this would be a ten and we'd all be under rocks by now.

"I'll drive the girls home. It's late."

Like docile little girls, Angelita and I follow King Khaled.

Angelita and I sit in the back seat of Khaled's car, which is nicer than the little white compact that Moktar drives.

"Mr. Al Kahairi, I was thinking of going on an excursion with the Geographic Society tomorrow. What do you think about that?"

"I understand that they are very educational, Kelly, and I know that they have the Authority's full approval."

"I'm going to call them and see if I can join them tomorrow."

"It's good to get out, Miss Day."

I'm dropped off first, Angelita checks for cats. It takes me a few minutes to locate the phone number of Dodge, the trip organizer.

Dodge answers on the first ring. "Yes, yes, please join us. We're going to have a wee bit of fun."

He talks extensively and enthusiastically about the itinerary. He's wearing me out.

"Thanks, Dodge, I'll see you in the parking lot. Good night."

I laugh to myself; even if I had the guts to sneak around like Inger, I couldn't rendezvous with Dan tomorrow because he's in jail. Poor Dan. I wonder how he's doing. I remember he told me once that because of his olive complexion and jet black hair he could pass for a Saudi and he often thought he was left alone when he otherwise might have been stopped. But I guess it didn't work Wednesday evening. Maybe he was targeted.

Chapter 14

Friday, September 25, 1987

It's loneliness that pushes me out the door of unit 5350 unescorted and into the unbearable heat at 7:00 in the morning. I'm on my way to join up with the Geographical Society. My goals are simple: abate my loneliness, get out of the dungeon, leave solitary confinement behind, and distract myself from my troubles. Oh yeah, and with the approval of the Authority, have an educational experience.

The meeting place is the hospital parking lot where a number of four-wheel drives are parked. Today's excursion is led by an intrepid spirit named Dodge, with whom I spoke last evening. Dodge is affable, five feet tall, blue-eyed and fiftyish. He's wearing hiking boots, baggy khaki pants, a brown and red plaid shirt, and a Caribbean pastel neckerchief that suggests colorblindness. A camera swings from a strap around his neck, and a baseball cap protects a balding scalp. He comes complete with scientific knowledge, plenty of history, some Arabic and a full bag of travel stories.

This group of expatriates is composed of the usual mix of nationalities: Italian, British, Irish, American, Scandinavian. Dodge reviews instructions on safety: tank-up, have plenty of water, use headlight signals when in trouble, keep first-aid kits handy for snake bites and the like. Then he gives us a skeleton itinerary which includes estimated travel time to various points and recommended vehicle speed.

It is so awful, I can't believe it. The way single women are allocated to the married couples. It's like that miserable feeling of being a wallflower at a high school dance and the discomfort of being the fifth wheel on a wagon. It's damn uncomfortable no matter how you slice it. At least Bev, in her quirky way, makes me feel needed when I'm out with her and Bob. The buffer for the strained marriage—at least it's a role. There are three of us single women. I can't tell if Dodge is asking or telling the couples who to take with them.

"Hi, I'm Kelly Day. I work over at the hospital."

A worn out white man says, "we're the Hanneys, Suzanne and Milfod." He tips his head towards the listless white woman at his side.

"Nice to meet you."

Milford says, "same here."

Suzanne nods her head as she looks me over.

Lastly, each vehicle is assigned its place in the convoy and with gusto, Dodge takes the lead in a red and white GMC High Sierra, and the convoy is off!

I decide if the Hanneys want to talk, it's their vehicle, and I am their guest so they'll have to take the lead on verbal exchanges. It might help if I could fall asleep. That way they could talk to each other and this trip, that I am now sorry I signed on for, would at least go faster. On the other hand, what would 5350, my little dungeon, offer me today? I could have stayed behind doors and listened to bootleg tapes of Maureen McGovern, Johnny Mathis, The Beatles, Phil Collins and the Eagles, eaten bland food and ruminated about my situation. This is the poison I've picked, so I'll look for something positive. I'll pretend I'm sleeping, and then eavesdrop on their conversation, if any. I'm pathetic. However, feigning sleep or actual sleep appeals to me now.

She whispers to him, "What's her name again?"

He whispers, "Kelly. Can't you even remember one name?"

Great, I'm not as welcome as the flowers in May. Maybe they just haven't had their morning coffee yet.

"We're stopping to stretch our legs," Suzanne's voice wakes me. I get out and grab my thermos from my bag. We're absolutely nowhere. Yep, that same blue sky and yellow road that brought me in from the Yanbu Airport.

I lose my resolve and break the silence. "I had a great nap," I say to Suzanne.

"You snore," she says. Then adds, "I wish I could nap." She's pushing sixty and her face is lined.

Milford joins us after he checks the engine. I'm wrong. Coffee does nothing for their collective mood. I ask a few questions. Their answers are clipped: Liverpool, three and a half years, geologic engineer, saving for retirement. I'm sorry I asked.

The other vehicles are also stopping. One of the rules about staying together. Now I see that every vehicle in the convoy does not have a married couple. Two vehicles are all males totaling seven guys. Dodge is at my side. He wants to know how I am enjoying the excursion. I'd be tempted to lie, but Milford and Suzanne are standing within earshot.

"I fell asleep. Can you believe that?"
"The terrain is smooth for now. It'll get bumpy about five kilometers from here," he says.

I offer him a peanut butter cookie from my snack pack. He accepts and goes to check on the rest of his flock.

Our travels take us way up steep inclines to picturesque rocky mountain tops and way down to dried river beds sprinkled with a few green-grey thorny bushes. We pass through tiny villages. We poke around the ruins of a settlement that was abandoned well over seventy years ago. We stumble upon a ruin that isn't yet listed in the Saudi Arabian book of antiquities. We climb a mountain to inspect at close range what is left of an old Turkish Fort. We stretch our legs at water wells, watch herds of straggly goats drink, and look on as tankers that haul water get filled. We lunch at the base of a gigantic sand dune that penetrates a cloudless blue sky. This uncultivated, uninhabited place is stunning.

After lunch, some of the men tell stories about working in Kenya, Libya, Yemen, Australia, and various regions of the Arabian Peninsula. Most of them are engineers of one kind or another. You name it: chemical, civil, mechanical, and so on. Have talent, will travel. I get the sense that they have no roots, no family ties, no religion or, country. I feel sad for and leery of these itinerant fellows. And, to think I felt rootless and without affiliation because I was on two different teams, unable to name my teammates in a softball season that was abruptly cut short. But I did come away with two base hits and drove one run home. Great stats.

The ride back to the hospital parking lot is quiet and uneventful. Suzanne and Milford drop me off at the hospital parking lot. We say our perfunctory farewells.

Then I thank Dodge for sharing his love of the desert. Thanks to him I was able to really see the desert. It is so much more than a blue ceiling and a yellow floor. Dodge offers to drive me home but I can't afford to take a chance. I walk to Camp Five and take consolation in the fact that it's still daylight.

I make a major project out of selecting my outfit for tomorrow. Change my mind several times. Finally decide on a long, flared-out A-line style periwinkle blue skirt, that I believe is the most figure-flattering in my collection, a white soft linen fitted blouse, and a white leather belt with a silver buckle. But, of course, the white hospital lab coat will hide the curves that I have. Pearl drop earrings and I'm done. Maybe in the morning, I'll try to jazz up my hair—just a little—French twist?

It dawns on me—I am looking forward to tomorrow and the presentation. I guess because the material I'm presenting is interesting—at least to me it is and I've been blessed—I'm not afraid to speak in public—I enjoy presentations—I enjoy debating—it's just the cat thing that's my Achilles heel.

One last thing before I try to get to sleep. I dial Dan's number, and let it ring twenty-five times. Then I say a prayer for him.

Chapter 15

Saturday, September 26, 1987

Khaled holds up the Saudi Gazette. The headline reads, "Ex-Pats Awash in Joy as King Fahad announces a retraction of the income tax decree." Khaled smiles, self-satisfied, like he knew all the while this was coming.

Rick says, "That's great. What's your reaction to the report?"

"I was just coming to that, Mr. Savage."

It seems to me King Khaled wants to remain awash in the joyous waters of the retraction a little while longer. It's like he wants to take some credit for the good news. It reminds me of the day he personally handed me my first piece of mail. He is a strange man—hard to figure yet there's a likeability about him.

"I think the report has substance. When we present this to Mr. Zahran, I'll take the lead and give him the big picture—an overview of our work," Khaled replies.

Sitting next to Rick, I can hear his breathing and feel his tension. I don't like this. We don't need a clash of egos at this juncture in the game.

Khaled again smiles a self-satisfied smile and rises from his chair. "I'll have Angelita call you when Mr. Zahran and I are ready to meet with you. I'm leaving now to pick him up from the airport." He walks with purpose as he exits the conference room.

. . .

Angelita phones me and says, "Mr. Rashid Zahran is here. Come to the conference room." She is smiling—I just know it.

Angelita serves us apple juice. Pleasantries are exchanged but they're a little stiff.

Mr. Al Kahairi does the introduction—the big picture thing. He gives the impression that he is the driving force behind this major project.

I report on surgery, labor and delivery, the emergency room, outpatient clinics, and inpatient units. If nurses work in the area, it belongs to me.

"I'd be happy to answer any questions, Mr. Zahran."

"I have none at this time. Thank you, Miss Day."

Next Dr. Small does the unexpected as he takes center stage. He says, "I'm as good at giving presentations as I am at dancing to a symphony." I laugh out loud and so does Mr. Zahran. I'm glad to see he has a sense of humor besides a nice face and a good education. Rick snickers. The puzzled look on Khaled's face is priceless.

Dr. Small reports on pharmacy, radiology, laboratory, and the medical records departments. His presentation is going well. He does not touch his ear—not even once. There are beads of perspiration just above his upper lip. The "I guess—I think" phrases creep in only now and then.

I observe Mr. Zahran engrossed in Rick's presentation. He is confident and energetic and doing a polished and bang-up job of reporting on maintenance and engineering, information systems, and purchasing.

Finally, Khaled presents the "big picture" again and summarizes the major findings. He is doing it with aplomb. I check for Mr. Zahran's reaction. He's listening. He does have a nice face. I wonder what he thinks of me.

At last, it's over. Mr. Zahran says, "I don't have any questions at this time. Thank you. Sorry, but I must run. I have a meeting in town."

Rick's sulkiness is palpable. He gets up, walks slowly to the conference room door, looks left and right down the corridor, returns to his chair and drops into it. He complains, "is that all Wonder Boy could say?"

"Yeah, I'm disappointed too. I thought we were good—I mean I think we were good," says Dr. Small.

"What do you think, Khaled?" I ask. He's on his feet and gathering up his papers.

"I believe the reports are substantive and the presentations good. My wife and I are hosting a dinner party for Rashid at my home tonight, so I'm sure he'll share his impressions with me then." He leaves.

"I feel a let down now," says Rick, "and I'm ticked off too. I've got so much fuckin' energy, I don't know what to do with myself—that was a big build up—a great report—and King Khaled will walk away with a trophy."

"Cool down, Rick, it's all a game. Mr. Zahran isn't stupid. Let Khaled have his day. I don't want any trouble with him. He got me out of jail and I owe him. All I want from this assignment is to do my job and return home safely."

"To a cat-free environment," he adds.

"Be quiet, Rick, I'm going to get over that—someday."

Dr. Small says, "Oh well," and picks up the phone on the side table and asks Angelita to make him a cup of hot tea.

I go to my office and stare at the postage stamp. My world is crazy. I'm very attracted to—correction—I lust after a handsome Mexican-American who's in jail in Yanbu, Saudi Arabia. Possibly the same cell I spent a night in for reasons of carrying a Louisville Slugger around with me. It was he who gave me the Slugger. I also find myself attracted to one Rashid Zahran of royal blood, Harvard educated, who wears a headdress and a robe, has a nice face, and a sense of humor.

I miss Fidelis—the soundest person I've met so far—and it's just about a week ago that she vanished. I'm surrounded by stray cats.

I pick up the phone and ask the switchboard operator to page Moktar for me.

"Hi, Kelly, you looking for me?"

"Got a minute?"

"Sure." He sits down.

"Are you curious about life in the West—the United States—England?"

He laughs. There's a long, long pause. I'm trying to imagine what he's thinking. Will he be open—honest? Does he know himself? Maybe he's too young to know himself.

"Sometimes, I wonder."

"I'm thirty-one. May I ask your age?"

He laughs again. "We're not as precise as—we don't celebrate birthdays here—only that of Mohammad. You must have noticed for medical records purposes—many of us have January 1 as our date of birth. Here's how it worked, after the question of—was the birth before or after Ramadan is asked of the parents, a physician examines the child and estimates the age. Now births are recorded. I know the exact ages of my children—unlike my parents. Times have changed. So, I'm somewhere around your age."

"I thought so. You have your family started—you know what kind of career you want, that's good—you love your faith …"

"Not so easy, Kelly. Westerners and their ways are a distraction—helpful, and distracting—and a temptation sometimes."

"Where did you learn to speak English so well?"

"That's a long story, Kelly."

"Tell me, please."

"I'll make it short."

"I'd prefer the long version."

"I was about three when I was diagnosed with a heart problem. I spent five years on a pediatric ward in the big hospital in Riyadh. I had operation after operation. Some successful—some not—repair, repeat, replace—you name it. The doctors and nurses became my family and one fantastic translator became my mentor. Majed, a Palestinian."

"On a Jordanian passport."

"Correct." He smiles. "But really I had many mentors—every nurse —every doctor—wanted to teach me something. So, I went to school in a pediatric ward under the tutelage of a large and diverse international faculty."

"That's fantastic. I think you learned a lot more than the ability to read, write and speak English."

"I did."

I think I heard a little bit of a choke in that deep guttural voice of his.

"How did you adjust when you came back here?"

"My parents thought I was odd and a little bit entertaining too. There were so many of us."

"Eight brothers, right? Nine kids counting you."

"Yes, you have a good memory, Kelly. Nine kids counting me."

We both hear his name called out on the overhead paging system— the hospital's school bell telling you recess is over, or it's time to change classes or go home.

For me, it's time to go to 5350, even though it's only 2:30. I'm spent.

.   .   .

I fix a light lunch and sit at the dining room table and write a long letter to my parents. I feel like a school kid writing an essay: What I did on my summer vacation.

I describe the strip mall and the seating arrangements in the Pizza Palace. I weave in the call to prayer and prayer time. I talk about the women and children's pool and elaborate on my brief career with the Women's Softball League—omitting the part about Dan, the Slugger, my incarceration, and now his incarceration. I don't mention the two trips to the Red Sea with Dan. It hurts me to think about it with Dan in jail.

Next, I list all the countries I can think of that the employees are from. I elaborate on the excursion into the desert with the Geographical Society. I paint the best picture I can.

Lastly, I ask them how they are doing knowing full well that they are burdened with my father's diagnosis of early stages of Alzheimer's.

His decline in driving skills is very sad and truthfully, dangerous. Taking the keys won't be easy. I seal the envelope.

I wander into the bedroom and stretch out on the lumpy bed and stare at the ceiling. I made the decision to take this job so far away from home. I know I wanted to leave Ashtabula not really because of the betrayal—the boyfriend and best girlfriend thing. I kind of put that out there—knowing that it was superficial—and the job loss—superficial too.

A small town can be cozy and comforting but for me it comes at a big price. Everyone knows your parents, everyone has expectations of you—teachers, neighbors—relatives. It's like a script has been written —with only minor variations. I was encouraged by the nuns to become a nun. My parents suggested nursing, lay teachers suggested teaching, and relatives more than hinted I owed my parents grandchildren.

On the other hand, it was my favorite aunt—Aunt Sheila Mary, a former Catholic nun who arranged for my adoption from an orphanage in Dublin, and whom we buried days before I left Ashtabula for this adventure who influenced me or at least gave me permission to create my own script. I knew I wanted to leave Ashtabula—not my parents. I wanted not to be so Catholic as well. I really didn't know what profession I wanted—so I became a nurse—part nun—part teacher—very Catholic—a parent pleaser and I could eventually marry and have children.

I look at Moktar and I admire him. I wanted to know if he longs for something else but I didn't want to be intrusive. Hopefully, in more conversations down the line, I'll get to know him better. I find him interesting and genuine. He knows his obligations to family.

Although I signed a contract for a year, I know my obligations to my parents. I'll take my R&R after six months and go home for a visit. In the meantime, frequent letters and phone calls are the order of the day. When my contract is up I will return home.

I can defer adventure and experiencing life—although I'm not really sure what I mean by that—specifically. I want to write the script or at least direct the play and I'm doing that now but with some pangs of conscience. Yet, I know obligations to my parents are also part and parcel of experiencing life—it is an adventure. We are primary to each other's life experience and adventure. We belong to each other. I drift off to sleep.

. . .

My phone rings. I drag myself to it. I check my watch—6:10 p.m.

"Kelly, how are you?"

"Well, Homer, what a surprise. I'm fine and how are you?"

"Great, great. I'm hosting a party tonight—I mean, no—I mean a quiet celebration. You know the retraction—income tax retraction thing—and, our great presentation to Mr. Zahran. We were good—you were good."

"But, oh, how—who?"

Homer interrupts, "Oh and most important—I've invited Khaled and Mr. Zahran."

"Really? Khaled said he was …"

Homer interrupts again, "Oh, I invited Khaled's wife too."

"Are they really planning on attending? Khaled said …"

"They're going to drop by after dinner—later."

"Homer, how are you … ?"

Again he interrupts, "Steve is helping me. Actually, he's arranged everything. Rick is helping out too."

He sounds nervous—but then he always does.

"What can I do to help?"

"Just bring your sweet self.

"Well, wait—if I get started now, I can make the one thing I'm good at—deviled eggs. But I don't know where you live?" I wait for a reply. I swear there is someone with him telling him what say.

"I'm picking you up. I'm picking you up at 9:00."

"But, Homer …"

Interrupts me again, "Kelly, we don't need eggs. It's being catered—our little quiet celebration.""Homer, are you sure this is all okay? You know how Khaled is about the rules and customs."

"Kelly, you wouldn't want to snub Mr. Al Kahairi and his wife—and what about Mr. Zahran? This will be a pleasant evening, I guess—I think."

"Okay. See you at 9:00." Even with help from Steve and Rick and catered food, I can't imagine him pulling off this quiet celebration or any event, really.

.   .   .

Dressed in my matching outfit of an ice-blue skirt and blouse and white pearl necklace, I'm poised to go to a gathering (quiet celebration) albeit empty-handed—eggless—waiting to be picked up.

I hear the toot of a horn at 9:15 p.m. In a flash, I'm out the door and into the back seat of a modest sedan on loan from the hospital to Dr. Small. We drive longer than I anticipated. "Say, Dr. Small, I mean, Homer, I didn't realize that you lived in the very fancy section of the married couples camp."

He laughs, turns his head and neck over his right shoulder to answer me. I don't trust his driving. That'll be my last comment.

"Well, Kelly, ah, the plan has been switched. It wasn't my idea."

"I can hear you—watch the road."

"Rick suggested that we switch the party—I mean the quiet celebration to where he's house sitting—bigger—nicer."

I maintain my silence even though I have a lot more questions. I don't want to wind up in the ER this evening alongside those other auto accident victims. I just want Homer to watch the road.

We pull into a circle drive—like something you'd see in Beverly Hills. The circle is jammed with cars. A valet, dressed like a bellhop from a movie in the thirties, requests the car keys. He looks familiar to me even though he's wearing an eye mask.

"Sunil?" asks Homer.

Sure enough, Sunil grins at both of us.

I have questions for Homer but before I get excited and jump to some wild conclusions—like this is the party that Steve's been planning all along—I'll hold my tongue

Homer presses the bell—we wait—he presses it again. I see he's nervous as his hand goes up to his ear and he avoids eye contact with me. I'm startled when Steve flings open the large wood carved paneled heavy door.

"Good evening dear guests," he shouts in a booming voice and his right arm thrusts upward and outward in an exaggerated welcoming gesture—that's not funny but grotesque.

He's wearing a tall pleated chef's hat which leans to the far left on his big head. His massive chest, arms and abdomen are snugly wrapped in a white double breasted chef's jacket trimmed in red and with two rows of gold buttons, many looking like they'll pop off any minute. White baggy pants complete the outfit that looks more like a Halloween costume than a uniform. He's even wearing an eye mask.

Small and I step into a two-story high foyer that's bigger than a bowling alley. An enormous crystal chandelier that must weigh a ton hangs high above our heads. If it dropped suddenly, it would kill all three of us instantly. A thundering crash and we'd be history.

We are enveloped in a sound system that prevents conversation so the chef imposter directs us with a sweep of his hand towards a winding grand staircase. My knees start to shake as we ascend the red thick carpeted stairs and I hear all too clearly, "Some say love, it is a river that drowns the tender reed. Some say love, it is a razor ..." from a million dollar sound system.

We arrive at the top of the stairs. Small is out of breath and I'm madder than hell. A poor imitation of "out of the age of opulence"—there is oversized and elaborate crown-molding, crystal drops dangling from an overabundance of sconces with colored light bulbs in the candle-shaped lamps. Despite six thick carved and closed wooden doors, the distinctive odor of marijuana permeates the air and the sounds of moans, groans, yelping, and frenzied laughter seep from under the big doors, conjuring up images of exciting, dangerous, and high voltage unrestrained indulgence. The chef imposter leans in towards a door and his big body jiggles. The corridor ends with another staircase and we descend into the living room and the chef imposter disappears.

This macabre costume party is in full swing. All the costumes are outrageous and exaggerated like Las Vegas show girls and carnival characters. There's a belly dancer, a bobby—a la London, an Elvis impersonator in a white jumpsuit with gold studs and a red and white cape. His wig is jet black and big—he's even carrying around a microphone. And, there's Little Bo Peep acting way out of character as she struts her stuff. There is not a thrown together get-up in this room. Lots of photos are being snapped—music blares, guys and gals dance. I don't recognize anyone—then there are a lot of rubber face masks, and eye masks.

There's a long busy bar at one end of the room with five bartenders serving up drinks. Small and I work our way to the other end of the room where a sumptuous buffet table including dozens of floral arrangements stretches for at least a mile.

My left hand hurts. I realize it's because I've been squeezing Homer's arm. I release my grip on him. He turns to me and says, "Kelly, I'm so sorry. They tricked me into this."

"Who's 'they' for God's sake?"

"Steve, Rick, Sunil, and some other guy I've never met before. I can't remember his name—a foreigner. Kelly, I must run to the little boy's room."

"Hurry—I'll wait right here, then we're leaving." I lean against a wall and survey the crowd hoping to see a familiar face—I do—Rick— he's dressed like a Roman Catholic priest—but with a patch over his right eye. He walks toward me.

"That's a good look for you, Rick."

"I thought so too, Kelly. You look like you're ready to make your first communion in your little skirt and blouse."

"Thank you. I'm surprised I was let in—but then there was no bouncer at the entrance—at least when I came in there wasn't. Where's Inger?"

"Waiting for me upstairs."

"Rick, I'm getting out of here as soon as Small returns."

He grins.

"Rick, did you have anything to do with tricking Homer into coming here?"

"Sort of." He winks with his left eye and saunters away.

"Hello," a male voice on my left startles me. I jerk my head towards him. It's Zynab.

"Oh, hi." He fits dressy casual to a tee—an expensive looking silk shirt, open collar, pressed slacks, and closed toe sandals. His dark sunglasses hint at Hollywood movie star impersonator.

"Nice to see you. I thought you didn't mingle?"

"I had no idea I was coming to a party."

He smiles a sickening smile.

Homer is at my side and he says, "Hello, I'm Homer," and extends his hand to Zynab.

I'm so furious, I look at Small and say, "I want to leave right now."

"I'll find Sunil and get the keys."

"Kelly, there's someone I want you to meet before you run off—stay right here." Zynab's voice trails off as he walks away.

Next, Jan and Carolyn appear. Jan's wearing a short tight strapless red dress, very red and very high heels, and a Tina Turner-like wig. She looks stunning. Carolyn is dressed like a rock star as well.

I blurt out, "I didn't know that this was going to be a party—I thought ..."

Zynab presents himself again and Carolyn and Jan walk away from us abruptly, never acknowledging Zynab. My heart almost stops—with Zynab is Tough Guy. Tough Guy takes a step towards me. He looks ridiculous in a ten gallon hat, a fringed vest, a pistol hanging on his belt, and cowboy boots complete with spurs. The smile on his face makes my skin crawl. I feel hemmed in by these two big thugs.

Zynab says, "Kelly, meet my cousin Akmed. But you know him, don't you?"

"Yes, I remember this guy." I stare into eyes that are circled by a mask.

Just then chef impersonator joins our little circle. "Akmed and I are old friends—from when I worked in Jeddah."

"So, you like to party, Akmed—and you like to dress like a cowboy," I say without thinking.

Zynab buts in, "You're here aren't you?"

"Just a minute," chef impersonator says. "We should all be civilized —it's a party, isn't it?"

"If we're going to be civilized then maybe this gunslinger here," I nod towards Tough Guy, "should have checked his pistol at the door."

I don't like them. I walk away and knock on what I believe to be a bathroom door.

"Just a minute."

I recognize Bev's voice. She flings the door open, I push my way in and close the door. Bev is dressed provocatively in a black evening gown—I guess she thinks she's a Hollywood star too.

"Bev, I need help—I need to get out of here. Where's Bob?"

"I'm not with him tonight."

"Bev, I'm scared—this is dangerous."

She laughs. "Relax. Have fun! Come and join me and Zynab."

Feeling outraged, I leave the bathroom and begin my search for Small. The music is loud and annoying—I push my way through the crowd and see the back of Small's head near the buffet. I rush to him —grab his elbow, "Homer, come on, we've got to get out of here."

I see Small has taken a break from his search for Sunil. He's got a plate of assorted appetizers in his hand. I could kill him.

"I couldn't find Sunil."

"Please, Homer, I need to get out of here. I'm really concerned. If you don't leave now, somehow I'll make it on my own."

"Okay, Kelly." He puts the plate on a side table.

We squeeze our way through a lively, loud, and vulgar collection of people. Out the front door and to the side of this big house—where we think the car might be parked—we see Sunil puffing on a cigarette. Small approaches him and asks for the keys and Sunil says, "I need to clear this with Steve."

Small grabs him by his collar with both hands, lifts him up off the ground, shakes him, and says, "Give me my keys."

Sunil surrenders the keys and runs away. Then Tough Guy comes from nowhere and grabs Dr. Small from behind. Small spins around and shoves Cowboy. Small moves in towards Cowboy.

"I'm a real cowboy—mister—I can rope a steer and tie a hog in a matter of seconds—stand back. I'm real good with my hands." He sounds like John Wayne.

Tough Guy doesn't look tough now. He walks away like the cowardly bully he is.

We have the car keys but we can see now that Small's car is boxed in.

He says, "We'll have to walk. I hope we can find our way."

"We will—let's go."

I turn and trip on a rock—hurt my knee—rip my skirt—soil my blouse. We're about three houses from the main street and Homer says, "Do you have your Igama?"

"Yes, I do, Homer." (I wanted to say, "Yes, John Wayne.") Both the Igama and the key to 5350 are tucked in my bra."

It's quiet and late—the temperature almost cool. We walk quickly down a very dark street—praying not to encounter a security patrol. I'm aware that I haven't seen a cat nor looked for one. That phobia takes a back seat to a much greater fear. My goal is to get to 5350 safely. We finally turn the corner into Camp Five.

Homer whispers, "I didn't get Cinderella home on time—it's after midnight, almost 1:00 a.m."

I'm keenly aware that I'm still not safely inside 5350 yet.

Chapter 16

Sunday, September 27, 1987

Walking towards 5350 in Camp Five, startled and confused, Small and I jerk our heads upwards to the night sky studded with a million stars.

"Did a jet just fly over? What was that sound?"

"A crash—a bomb—something big—I don't know, Kelly."

We don't talk, we save our breath and run to the hospital. The still night air is heavy with a peculiar odor. My thoughts are racing in all directions.

We arrive at the emergency room. Restrained panic is written all over Moktar's face. Small, myself, and a skeleton crew of night staff stand close to Moktar.

"We just got the call from the local Civil Defense office—there's been an explosion at the refinery. We can expect thirty some victims —burns and smoke inhalation. An estimate of six very serious burns should arrive first. These numbers are preliminary, of course."

My heart sinks—my throat tightens. Dan—he's safe in jail. I thank God and hold back tears. There's work to do.

It's 1:15 and Dr. Small announces on the overhead system: "attention please, operation triage—mass casualties disaster plan is in effect."

Per plan, I dash to my office and get the list of staff phone numbers. I put check marks by names, assign a nurse's aide to use my office phone to make the calls and I return to the ER.

Mr. Al Kahairi and Mr. Zahran come rushing into the emergency room. Khaled is breathing hard and sweating. Rashid maintains his usual reserve.

Khaled says, "I was called minutes ago, at home. How did you …"

Dr. Small interrupts Khaled and ignores what is an obvious and logical question.

"Operation triage—mass casualties disaster plan is in effect. Three ambulances and one hospital bus, along with three doctors and nurses have been dispatched to the refinery. We won't see a victim until triage is completed. Some critical care will be initiated on site. We've got about a forty minute window before we see our first victim come thru those doors."

No stammering—all spoken with speed and clarity.

Khaled says, "I know my responsibilities. I'll start the communications with the Authority. Where's Rick?"

Dr. Small and I look at each other.

"What's wrong?" Khaled asks.

"He's house sitting in the married couples camp. We don't have a phone number," I say.

Dr. Small stammers and volunteers, "But, but, I know the address."

"Fine, I'll send Security to pick him up."

I look down at the floor.

"What is it, Miss Day?"

Homer answers for me. "There's a big party ..."

Khaled's face reddens, his jaw is set. If it wasn't for Mr. Zahran standing by, I think Khaled would knock Homer's head and mine together and demand some answers. Why does Homer look disheveled and why does Kelly have on a soiled blouse and a ripped skirt? Why are they both at the hospital at 1:25 in the morning?

I thank God he's afraid of our answers for fear Mr. Zahran might think he's not minding the store if his top level staff are gathering, partying, and mingling behind his back. I won't blame him if, at a later day, he does bang our heads together.

Khaled says, "I'll send Security and I'll tell them to bypass the police station and bring him straight here. We have our priorities."

"Mr. Al Kahairi, if Steve is there, we'll need him too."

I look to Mr. Zahran and say, "he's our emergency room manager."

I don't need to put a bid in for Carolyn. I'm confident there's no near term pregnant woman working at the refinery. We could use Inger's help but I rationalize she'll know about the disaster shortly. She's clever enough to make a plan. I can't make a bid for Jan, as she could be drunk by now and knowing how she's dressed—well.

Dr. Small says, "I'm going to head for the outpatient clinics and with the help of one of the nurses, we'll prepare to treat the walking wounded who will arrive on the hospital bus from the refinery. When Rick gets here, he'll manage supplies and traffic control in the hospital and in the parking lot. When Angelita gets here, she'll maintain a record of the events as they unfold."

Moktar says, "I'll organize the main lobby as the holding area for the families and friends of victims, as soon as I get back from Camp Five with a bus full of nurses.

I look at Mr. Zahran and say, "we all know our roles as they are clearly stated in the disaster plan."

Mr. Al Kahairi says, "I've got to get the communication going with the Authority. Let's meet in the conference room after the first victims arrive and treatment has begun and remember to use the two-way radios as planned—Security is Channel one—we're on two. Telephone lines should be used sparely."

Mr. Zahran says, "I will spend time with each of you during the critical period. Miss Day, I will be with you first."

"That works for me." Damn it, I should have said that differently.

Mr. Al Kahairi and Dr. Small dash off.

.   .   .

The dreadful calm laced with tension in the ER as the staff stand by in anticipation of the arrival of our first victims, is interrupted at 1:55 a.m. by Steve, dressed as a chef, minus the outlandish chef's hat, Rick dressed in a black shirt, minus the white Roman collar, and black trousers. Inger wearing a dress that's too big for her—but at least it covers most of her arms and hangs below mid-calf. It's the pink leather high heels that look silly. I'm just guessing but I think she outfitted herself from the closet of the woman who's having a swinging time in Bali. I admire her—she's here—she's got guts. Mr. Zahran and I approach them.

"I'm glad you're here. You've got time to change into scrubs."

Mr. Zahran adds, "You're needed."

At 2:08, the acrid odor of burnt flesh precedes the three gurneys that roll into the ER, bodies badly charred. The staff swing into action with a high level of energy: constant, focused on supporting life, relieving pain and suffering.

. . .

It's 2:45. Dr. Small, Khaled, Rick, and I, with Mr. Zahran at my side, meet briefly to update each other and re-assess our situation. We've asked Moktar and Angelita to join us, and they do.

Dr. Small says, "As we already know, three more serious burns are on the way. The bus will be arriving very soon with exactly twenty-seven walking wounded, half of them likely to require at least an overnight stay. Intravenous therapy for at least a dozen victims is anticipated."

We all agree that to be safe, back-up staff from the hospital in Taif should be requested and that is my responsibility. Rick, Moktar, and Angelita are quiet but very attentive.

Mr. Al Kahairi says, "the Authorities have been informed of our current status and are prepared to support whatever needs we have. And one more thing, the airport has been closed down and selected roads have been blocked. It is just a precaution, I assure you. I'll call a meeting around 4:00, or sooner if indicated. Thank you."

. . .

Before Mr. Zahran and I go to my office to call Taif, I say, "we'll make a quick stop in the ER."

It's noisy, loud and crowded. Correctly identifying victims and getting basic information is challenging. Women are weeping, doctors are shouting orders in English and Arabic. Stretchers and wheelchairs line the main corridor. Supply carts and medical equipment are scattered from one end of the ER to the other.

"How are you holding up, Inger?"

"I'm a little weary. It was the most horrific ... then giving the family the news—well, you know. Moktar is still with the family."

"You need a break, Inger."

"I promise I'll take one later."

Mr. Zahran thanks Inger.

. . .

We walk in silence to my office. I dial up the home of the administrator at the hospital in Taif, and I explain our situation to him. I request two surgeons, a pulmonary specialist, and three critical care nurses. I can expect one surgeon, one pulmonary specialist, two critical care nurses, and ten trays of instruments to be used in debridement of dead tissue from burns, and twenty-four bottles of intravenous fluids. Estimated time of arrival between 4:00 and 5:00 a.m. Best they can do.

Mr. Zahran uses my phone to call Riyadh. He arranges for the road block to be lifted for the entourage arriving from Taif. Then I suggest we make a quick tour of the critical areas.

. . .

The hospital is filling up with security personnel, men from the Authority, and families of victims. At 3:06 the bus arrives from the refinery, unloading victims at the outpatient department.

On the inpatient units, the doctors and nurses have identified patients who can be discharged now in order to free up beds: families are being contacted to come and get them. If they don't have a family, or the family has no phone, we'll have them get dressed and sit in the lobby—we'll feed them breakfast in the morning, and then organize transportation for them.

I explain to Mr. Zahran, "Comfort areas for staff are being set up now—two male rooms and four female rooms. Some rooms are for staff to eat, drink, and have a chance to support each other. The other rooms are for rest and sleep. The rooms will be ready by 4:00—when we'll be close to three hours into this disaster."

We return to the ER—where the command post has been established. "Steve, you need a break. Steve, you need to take one now. You don't look well at all; I'm concerned."

Steve collapses right in front of me. I shout for a code to be called and I start mouth-to-mouth resuscitation. Steve's blue. Intubation is successful. His heart is shocked twice. It beats on its own now, and in the skilled hands of Inger, medications are pushed into his system by intravenous injections. We lift Steve from the floor to a gurney—requiring six of us. From here he'll be wheeled straight into the Cardiac Care Unit.

Inger is dripping with sweat. I grab her hand and lead her to a chair. She's dazed.

"Was he in the explosion?"

"Inger, do you know where you are?" I ask.

"Was he in the explosion?"

"Inger, you just helped resuscitate Steve. You, me, and the code team."

Mr. Zahran at my side, says, "What do you need?"

"Rick needs to be here." He leaves and returns with Rick.

"Rick, take her to a quiet place. My office is open. She's a little confused. I'll join you shortly."

Again Mr. Zahran is at my side like a sentry. The expression, "strong silent type," fits him well. I feel supported and not at all uncomfortable, even though I'm being observed by a superior during a crisis. He's got a talent. More executives should have that talent.

I grab BP equipment and an apple juice. We go to my office. Inger is withdrawn. She is mumbling something about the burn victims. When she stops, I check her vital signs. They're good. I give her the apple juice. Rick holds her hand. He looks terrified.

"She's going to be okay, Rick. She's resilient. You know that." A hint of a smile crosses the sentry's face.

"I'll walk her to a comfort station and then I'll meet you two in the conference room."

.   .   .

It's 4:00 and Mr. Al Kahairi asks the team, "Where do we stand? And, Angelita, please take detailed notes."

I report first: "as you've already heard—I'm sure—we've lost our first patient—he died on the stretcher that he was rolled in on—he didn't have a chance. Since then three firemen have been admitted with smoke inhalation. And, I'm sorry to report Steve's in Cardiac Care—you've probably already got this bad news as well. I just left Inger at the women's comfort station. She's in shock but already on the mend. We need the Taif crew badly."

"Did Steve have a heart attack?" Khaled asks.

"Well, his heart stopped—we got it restarted—it's a heart rate—rhythm problem—so far as we know right now."

Dr. Small's eyes meet mine. I know what he's thinking—substance induced cardiac arrhythmia.

Then Dr. Small says, "The walking wounded are being managed. We've been lucky that nothing major has come through the ER. I mean, other than the victims from the refinery. You know what I mean."

"We understand that," says Khaled.

"Moktar, what's your perspective on the situation?" I ask.

"We always have car accident victims on the evening shift—some during the night. None yet, however. Some families don't have phones, so there will be a lag time before they find out about the explosion. When they do—or if their sons don't come home on time from the refinery—they'll pile in cars. Whole families. They will head for the hospital driving like crazy. There's going to be accidents."

Rick says, "Thanks, Khaled, for keeping the security personnel and the authority out of the clinical areas. There is congestion, but the confusion is being kept to a minimum. There are no problems so far in the parking lots."

"The good news is that staff from Taif are due in soon. I agree with Moktar—the car accidents will come," I say.

Then Dr. Small adds "I'm glad you requested the additional intravenous fluids from Taif, Kelly—I'll need them. Thanks for anticipating that. I can say, however, we've got plenty of antibiotics on hand."

We all chuckle.

Mr. Zahran puts his hand on Homer's shoulder and says, "thank you, Dr. Small, your dark humor is appreciated."

Khaled says, "the Authority says the fire is beginning to get under control. Keep up the good work. We'll get updated and reassess in an hour, or sooner if needed. Mr. Zahran, I'd like you to join me now in my office with the Authority. We have some other pressing issues."

.   .   .

I'm relieved to have a break from Mr. Zahran. I hope the Authority keep him involved for a long time. I'm exhausted and I think I'm starting to stink.

I go to the administrative office and find Angelita typing away.

"Angelita, I'll get a driver for you. Here are my keys. I need a change of clothes—pick anything out—underwear is in a drawer, my shampoo, my hair dryer, a hairbrush, and my makeup you'll find on the sink in the bathroom."

"Consider it done, Kelly. He's nice, isn't he?"

"Yes, Angelita, he is."

She has no idea how lucky she is that she wasn't at the orgy last night. I am so fearful of the fallout.

.   .   .

It's 4:20 and my two-way radio calls me to go back to the ER. The Taif staff have arrived. A briefing is done and assignments are made. They're eager to help—soon they'll have the situation in hand. More staff will get breaks. I'm guardedly optimistic that we'll get through this.

.   .   .

I go to my office and close the door—I need privacy. I take a deep breath, put my hand on the phone.

"Carolyn—it's me. Are you safe?"

She sobs, "I'm okay. It was a mess."

"Carolyn, tell me only what I need to know now."

"Jan's in jail—I don't know how many others. Drugs were found."

"I'm sorry about Jan."

"Am I needed—I know about ..."

"No, come to work as usual. Good-bye."

.   .   .

With a bag of fresh clothes, I head for the women's ward to find an available shower. The grime, the sweat, and the odors are off my body but my head is a cluttered mess—fear, anxiety, concerns. I'm scared as hell. I make rounds in my areas and take notes, while giving directions and support as needed.

.   .   .

It's 6:00. Khaled reports first. "The fire at the refinery is under control. Obviously, investigations are underway. The airport will remain closed as well as selected roads."

I report, "the five major burn victims remain serious, but are in stable condition. Steve's not doing well—he's in and out of consciousness. No visitors please. Inger has recovered and is on her way to Camp Five for a rest. We did get car accidents as Moktar predicted—thankfully mostly minor stuff. And, thanks to Mr. Zahran's intervention, the administrator at the Taif Hospital will allow us to keep their staff for another forty-eight hours."

I'm distracted and nervous and don't really hear Small's or Rick's reports. Angelita says, "Will somebody declare the disaster over before my hand falls off?"

"The disaster is officially over," announces Mr. Al Kahairi.

Mr. Zahran adds, "the team functioned well. My thanks to all of you."

.   .   .

I get up and walk quickly to my office.

I stare at the postage stamp. I think about Dan in jail, the victims, the exhausted firemen, the distressed families in the lobby, and Steve in Cardiac Care hanging on to his life by a thread—his connection to Tough Guy—Tough Guy's connection to Zynab. That fucking party! I feel like a big fool—so damn stupid. And then there's Mr. Zahran, who taps on my office door.

"May I come in?"

"Yes." I almost jump out of my chair.

His deportment is grave. He sits down. My heart sinks to my stomach.

"Miss Day, you are being expelled immediately."

"I ..."

"I'll explain. Mr. Al Kahairi, as your sponsor, has the authority to expel you from employment. I persuaded him to do so. This is your chance to avoid arrest, possibly physical harm—at best a lengthy deportation hearing—at worst death."

"I don't ..."

"Miss Day, you have to trust me."

"I want to."

"You could be charged with any of the following: indecent dress, consumption of alcohol, association with males to whom you are not related and worst case scenario—charged with prostitution. The Commission on the Promotion of Virtue and the Prevention of Vice are out in full force as we speak. We must move fast to avoid arrest."

"You're telling me I don't have a choice."

"Miss Day, you have no choice in this matter. Listen carefully, we don't have much time. I have your passport on me. I need it to make your travel arrangements. Do you know how to get to the loading dock from inside?"

I nod. "Through the laundry."

"Moktar is waiting for you there. He'll drive you to a place—don't share any information with him. He will not ask you any questions."

• • •

I take my small purse from the lower desk drawer, hide it inside my lab coat under my arm, look at the postage stamp for the last time. I put my bag of dirty clothes in the wastebasket and get a lump in my throat.

I lock my office door and walk, not too quickly or too slowly, past the administrative offices. Dr. Small is coming towards me.

"Kelly, got a minute?"

"Not now, Homer, believe me, I've got my hands full." I quicken my pace.

"It'll just take a minute …"

I gesture with a wave of my hand and shake my head. I make it to the noisy and warm laundry—washers churning and dryers spinning —I see Fidelis' alcove in the distance—for a fraction of a second I thought I saw her sitting at her desk. I smell lemongrass. I shake myself.

• • •

Moktar says only one thing. "Lie down in the back seat so not to be seen."

We ride for about twenty minutes and stop. I hear another car pull up. Moktar says, "Kelly, get out on the left side and get in the limo. Inshallah."

My throat is so tight I can't speak. The sun is blazing and hurts my eyes. A black limousine with an open door is six feet from me. I get in the back seat. Mr. Zahran is seated in the front with the driver. The windows are tinted.

"Try to get some sleep, Miss Day. We'll be on the road for some time." A shield between me and the two men goes up. I remove my lab coat and wrap my small purse in it and put it under my head. I'm in and out of sleep and nightmares plague me.

The limousine stops. I hear Mr. Zahran talking but I can't make out what he's saying. Another male voice is talking excitedly in both English and Arabic. The shield never goes down but the door on my right is opened.

"Good afternoon, Miss Day, please follow me. We must hurry." He looks very official in a Saudi Airline uniform. I realize that I'm in Jeddah where I see the enormous illuminated sign: Welcome to King Abdul Aziz International Airport. I'm almost running to keep up with this long-legged young man. I'm several steps behind him and short of breath. I don't take my eyes off him. In my peripheral vision I have fleeting images of security guards—every one of them looks like Tough Guy. The tall man escorts me onto a jumbo jet and seats me in the first class section. The steward is watching us carefully.

"Miss Day, I hope you enjoyed your stay in the Kingdom—Inshallah." And then he dumps my passport, travel documents, and a white business envelope with only "Miss Day" on the front into my lap and he's off the airplane.

The steward recites the usual script. I learn that I'm headed for a brief stopover in Rome, then on to London where this flight terminates. Once I'm airborne, I'll open the white business envelope.

.   .   .

Mr. Zahran has taken care of everything. I follow his instructions to the letter and take a taxi to 53 Park Lane, Mayfair, London. A tall clean shaven, graying at the temples doorman greets me. "Good evening, madam, welcome to the Dorchester Hotel."

Next, a dapper young bellman looks at me with a question mark on his boyish face. I shake my head and mumble, "No luggage."

Next a well-groomed and efficient clerk from behind an elegant desk says, "Welcome, Miss Day, we've been expecting you. Richard will escort you to your suite, The Belgravia."

Although I'm not dressed for the part, I feel like royalty as I'm swept through the massive and gorgeous lobby. The air is perfumed and intoxicating.

My parents' home could comfortably fit in the foyer of the Belgravia Suite. Richard points out the sitting area, bedroom, bath, and balcony where he says, "you'll enjoy a magnificent view of Hyde Park in the morning."

A doorbell rings—Richard attends to the door. A cart is rolled in. "We've taken the liberty of preparing a late supper for you," he says.

Cheeses, grapes, apples, crackers, assorted meats are beautifully displayed. Richard, without asking, uncorks a bottle of red wine and pours a glass. "Have a good night's rest, Miss Day. Anything I can do for you before I leave?"

"Yes, the time please."

He pulls a timepiece from his vest pocket, studies it, looks up and smiles. "Miss Day, it's 11:57 precisely—Greenwich Mean Time."

"Thank you, Richard, you've been most kind."

Chapter 17

Monday, September 28, 1987

In a big bed in a big room, I wake up with a start. My heart is racing. I don't know where I am. "Think," I tell myself. My breathing is shallow and rapid. The bed covers are warm, light-weight and soft. The room has a floral scent.

As my eyes accommodate to the darkness, my heart begins to slow. A lamp and a phone are on the bedside table. Raising my head and leaning on my elbow, I fumble with the lamp switch, hit the operator button on the phone and wait.

"Hello, Miss Day, welcome. It's lovely that you've arrived."

My heart rate picks back up and my stomach does a flip-flop. I know that voice—I've heard it before.

"Miss Day, how may I be of assistance to you? Miss Day, are you alright?"

"I … I, excuse me, I thought you were someone I knew."

"Miss Day, what do you need?"

"Where am I?" I think I know but I need her to tell me.

"The Dorchester Hotel."

"The time?"

Three-thirty-three a.m. precisely."

"The date?"

"Monday, 28 September, 1987. Do you need anything, Miss Day, anything at all?"

"No, thank you—sincerely. I really mean sincerely."

My head falls back on the pillow—the receiver slips from my hand. For a brief moment, I thought it was Carolyn who was on the other end of the line and I was back in Unit 5350. I feel old and tired, yet young, and relieved.

I want to get up and make sure I'm locked in but my legs won't accept the command. I fall back to sleep only to wake up with a start again—less frightened but having no idea how long I've slept.

I try again to command my legs—the circuits are slow. I concentrate—I'm finally upright. I stagger to the bathroom. I splash cold water on my face, look in the mirror, recognize myself, and fully realize I'm alive and in London, England. I see my skirt and blouse are on the floor in a heap.

I pull a big towel from a fancy rack, wrap it around me and go to find the door that I must have entered through last night and double lock it. I draw the heavy drapes, open a door and step out onto the spacious balcony overlooking the Hyde Park. I pull the big towel tight around my shoulders. The morning air is chilly and heavy with mist— the sky is grey. The park is rich with many shades of green with hints of changes in little bits of autumn yellow, red, orange, and gold.

I linger on the balcony and cherish my life, freedom, and the good deed done to me by Mr. Zahran.

Sufficiently chilled to the bone, I take a long hot shower in the spacious black marble bathroom, get dressed, sit at the table, and eat some fruit and cheese. It must have been me who drank the wine last night—there's one used glass and a bottle half empty.

I call my parents and tell them I'm vacationing in London. Mom's thrilled for me and tells me to be sure to see the Crown jewels and the Changing of the Guard. Dad says he's going to the hardware store. She takes back the phone from him. We both know he's confused. I promise to call again in a few days.

Next, I hit the operator button, get the time and change my watch and the lovely voice volunteers, "If you are going out, please take the umbrella provided for you from the cupboard as a bit of a drizzle is expected."

I walk for over two hours in a bit of a drizzle. I go over and over every encounter I've had with Mr. Zahran. I believe that I can recall every word he has ever said to me.

I stop for tea and rest. I ask the waitress to direct me to a moderately priced dress shop. In a Cockney accent that I wish I could mimic, she entertains me with her description of the Liberty Department Store on Regent Street. A creaky 1920's mock Tudor masterpiece with up-market fashions and a respectful dressmaking heritage. I purchase a simple, black dress, V-neck with cap sleeves, black pumps, a black shawl with speckles of silver, and a hunter green wool crepe dress, sweetheart neckline, fitted at the waist, short straight skirt.

I come upon an Indian restaurant and feel compelled to enter. When my friends and I would go to Cleveland to visit the art museum at University Circle, we always stopped at an Indian restaurant afterwards. I search the lengthy menu for some of my favorite comfort foods. A chicken curry dish, a side of boiled red lentils, and a small cucumber salad deliver on the promise of sublimely aromatic and divinely flavorful. I'm relaxed. I think about Mr. Zahran.

Back at the Dorchester, I find the message light flashing. I carefully follow the directions to pick up messages.

"Miss Day, I hope you are getting your needed rest. I'll call you in the morning. My flight gets in early. Let's meet for breakfast. Sleep well." I play the message three times. I love the sound of his voice.

I toss and turn in the splendid big bed. Unable to sleep, I get up and review the instructions that were dropped into my lap by the Saudi Airline employee. I will be here at the Dorchester for two more nights, Tuesday, the 29th and Wednesday the 30th. I take off for New York on Thursday. I help myself to the honor bar. They're small so I take two Hennesseys and pour them over ice and turn on the telly. I pay no attention to it. It's some late night talk show. I think about Mr. Zahran and promise myself that I am not going to fall in love with him. I'm simply going to enjoy his company.

Chapter 18

Tuesday, September 29, 1987

"Yes, I'm fine—relaxed—rested. I slept well, thank you."

"Good. Ready for breakfast? I know it's early, but I'm anxious to see you."

"It's fine. I'm an early riser. Sure—lobby in ten minutes." I'm so nervous—I don't know what to expect. If this elevator doesn't come soon I'll take the stairs. This is nerve racking. He's just a guy for heaven's sake. I scan the lobby. Oh my God, I almost don't recognize him. I didn't expect to see him in Western-style clothes and certainly not jeans and a leather jacket. He's not looking this way. I take a minute to compose myself and slowly walk towards him. I am near when he turns his head in my direction. His smile weakens my composure.

"Hi."

"Hi," I say just above a whisper and feel my face flush. We don't touch. I'm glad because my hands are sweaty and a little shaky. I'm happy he's chatty because I'm afraid to speak.

"Are you okay, Miss Day?"

"Yes, I'm fine," my voice squeaks.

"Really, Miss Day, are you okay?"

"I'm nervous. Frankly, I'm out of my element here. You look very nice by the way." I refrain from saying, "that's a nice hair cut."

"And you look lovely."

I pick at the eggs and don't lift the coffee cup because I'm shaky and afraid I'll spill it. The glass with orange juice is safer; it's small and only half full. I sip it.

"We have some business, Miss Day, but it can wait. I want to show you around town. I'm your personal tour guide for today. May I call you Kelly?"

"Sure."

"And you'll call me Rashid?"

"Sure."

"I'll get an umbrella from my room—just in case. Did you need to go upstairs?"

"Yes, I want to brush my teeth." If I don't relax and lighten up he'll be sick of me in less than an hour. He's so worldly and comfortable here.

We get on the elevator and he pushes the seventh floor button. He says, "I'm in a suite at the other end of the hall from yours."

"Oh."

"See you in the lobby in ten."

"Sure." My vocabulary is unbelievably limited on this Tuesday morning at the Dorchester in London in the company of a very sophisticated man who is related to the King of Saudi Arabia.

I brush my teeth and put a second coat of mascara on my lashes, freshen my lipstick, and play with my hair. I check my wrist watch a hundred times—twelve minutes have passed. Oh, God, there he is by the elevator.

"Perfect timing," he grins.

"Indeed," I smile.

"You tell me—Marble Arch, Hyde Park, Kensington Gardens, or Picadilly Circus, Chinatown, Covent Garden in the other direction."

"Definitely Covent Garden." I have no idea why I said that.

"Let me know if you want to go into the shops."

"Oh no, I'm not a shopper. I just want to walk. It's all so exciting and I want to hear your commentary." Calm down, Kelly.

"This is my favorite city in the world." Favorite city implies familiarity with many cities. He weaves up and down quaint narrow lanes. There's not a man in all of Ashtabula that could begin to compare to him. He's really something. And I need to get a grip. Picadilly Circus is over-stimulating. I am at baseline over-stimulated on this beautiful morning. Rashid is enthusiastic about everything—pointing out attractions and places of interest that we'll visit tomorrow if I'd like. He refers to today as an overview of the attractions. For me, he is the attraction. All the other stuff is—I don't know what it is.

"Ready for lunch? You must be hungry, you didn't touch your breakfast."

"Yeah, I am. I can't believe it's one o'clock. The time is going so fast."

"Inside or out?"

"Either is fine." I should have committed to one or the other. I'm so bland. I'm starting to bore myself.

As we wait to be served steak and kidney pie (Rashid's recommendation), he begins the business part.

"Kelly, I believe that Steve, with some help from Rick, tricked both you and Dr. Small into going to that awful party." He pauses.

I dive in, "Yes, of course, that's what happened." The pitch and intensity of my voice surprises me.

"Now that's behind you."

"Thanks to you." He seems to close doors quickly. Possibly he's not interested in my story. He probably has heard enough ex-pat stories to last a lifetime.

"Please enjoy the next few days—relax and have fun. If I crowd you —just tell me. I realize we don't know each other very well. I thought it best that you rest up some place nice before returning to Ashtabula, Ohio. It's a long trip."

"I agree. I need to recuperate. It's been a very eventful and disconcerting three weeks." I'm surprised that he knows exactly where I'm from. That's a level of detail that I would not expect him to have.

"Eventful?"

"Well, yes, the refinery explosion, the party and other stuff."

"Like?"

"The refinery explosion is only one thing. You know, had you not asked me about disaster preparedness on our first meeting—I doubt we could have been so ready. That was sheer luck—we could have lost way more than one life that night. And if you weren't there to facilitate the swift arrival of the Tiaf staff—with the roads blocked and all, we'd have been in big trouble."

His demeanor changes as he shifts in his chair. He looks away.

"Yes, quite a coincidence."

The pie is served. "It's comforting just to look at it—that golden crust is beautiful." I need to calm down—it's not like I've never seen a golden pie crust before.

Rashid chuckles. "This restaurant does not serve pork in the pie, but chunks of beef, lamb kidneys, fried onions and brown gravy with a touch of Guinness. I enjoy the aroma as much as the taste."

Thank God for food—it does so much more than nourish the body. It's a wonderfully safe subject. I'm starting to relax. Rashid seems to be enjoying this safe space because he is now elaborating on the prep time, cooking time, and various ingredients that can be added. I tell him about my mother's chicken pot pie.

"Can you make it as well as your mother?"

"Yes, yes I can." I just told him a big fat lie. Oh, hell with it—I want to impress him—it's just a small fib. He'll never know—I'll never see him again after the next few days.

"Kelly, something wrong?"

"No." I lie again. The thought of never really getting to know him is very sad for me. Does he care that we'll never meet again after this?

"There is something that I'd like to share with you. But let's finish our meal—the tables are so close here and this is a very private matter."

He looks alarmed. Now we're silent. My stomach is in knots. I think I said something to spoil his mood. What is my need to push to share and ask questions when it seems clear he's not interested?

We start our walk back to the hotel. I tell him that I arrived at the King Abdul Aziz International Airport in Jeddah in enough time to make my connecting flight to Yanbu, but the "handlers" of this single women messed up. I give him the whole story of my night in the airport and detail the incident with Tough Guy.

Rashid lets out a heavy sigh, shakes his head but says nothing.

Why I am telling him all this—I'm getting out safely thanks to him. What difference does all this make now? Yet, I want, so desperately, his take on my experience.

Walking in an uncomfortable and stiff silence, it starts to rain. He opens the umbrella, puts his arm in mine and pulls me close to him. To think of how light-hearted we were over breakfast and now we're somber.

He stops and says, "Let's get out of the rain and get a cup of coffee."

We settle into a quiet corner booth—place our order with a waitress who cracks gum like it was an art form. We both chuckle. I want to kiss her for breaking the tension.

"What are you thinking, Kelly?"

I hesitate for a long time. I wish Fidelis were here to advise me. For some reason it nags me that he presented such an over-simplified explanation—that Steve tricked me and Homer into going to a party. Is he so naïve? Why didn't he ask my opinion about what happened?

"Kelly?"

"I'm thinking."

"Okay."

"Here it is." I connect the dots: Zynab at the Big Bun attempting to pick me up, Zynab at the women's softball game, Zynab at the infamous party, Zynab connected to Steve. Zynab claiming that he and Tough Guy are cousins. Tough Guy shows up at the infamous party and has a fistfight with Homer. I'm watching for Rashid's reaction.

He looks stunned and worried. It's like I've given him some bad news.

I was going to tell him about my night in jail but that seems like a minor and unnecessary detail about my brief stay in Yanbu in light of the refinery explosion and the infamous party.

Finally, he says, "Kelly, I'm sorry. I don't know what to say."

My sense of it is that he's not willing to share his thoughts. Or maybe he just doesn't give a damn and I'm boring him.

We taxi back to the Dorchester and ride the elevator to the seventh floor. We step out into the magnificent and silent corridor. Rashid stands very close to me, his dark eyes are sad, his face is tight. "Kelly, give me your passport."

"But, I can take care of myself now. I don't understand why …"

"I can make things happen faster."

"You're scaring me, Mr. Zahran—faster?"

"Please, trust me."

I hesitate, dig in my purse, and hand over my passport reluctantly. I watch the back of his head—he walks briskly down the hall. I watch him enter his suite.

.   .   .

I walk slowly to my suite and fumble with the key. I'm trembling all over. I hear a noise coming from the bathroom. "Who's there?" I screech. A maid shows her head.

"I'm sorry, I'm sorry. Would you please leave and come back later?"

"Yes, of course."

It seems like an eternity before she gathers up her cart and materials. She looks over her shoulder at me and closes the door behind her.

I place my few belongings in a Liberty department store bag. I pace around the suite. I'll call the American Embassy. That's what I'll do. What will I tell them? I handed my passport over to a stranger, lost it, somebody must have stolen it … Starting with a lie is not a smart idea. I'll walk to wherever the Embassy is, go in and tell my story. I've done nothing wrong.

If only I knew one person in this vast city. I have a credit card. I can go and hide in a small hotel and take some time to think. Why didn't I push Rashid for more discussion—answers? He seems quite eager to get me on my way now. Why? And why doesn't he have more questions for me?

The phone rings—I stare at it—with a sweaty hand I pick up the receiver.

"Miss Day, you are all checked out and your driver is here." She sounds like Carolyn which brings back a flood of memories about my first meeting with her and Jan and all their stories and warnings.

"Thank you." I don't like this and I'm scared. The elevator ride is too fast. No stops. The length of the lobby too short. The doorman calls me by name and opens a limo door and I slip in the back seat next to Rashid. He looks sad, and his skin ashen.

He says, "You're on your way home—Heathrow, JFK, Cleveland. He puts my passport and tickets in my hand. You'll be home tonight."

After a while he puts his arm around me. I can hardly breathe. I have so many feelings—all fighting and arguing with each other. I start to criticize myself for I don't know what. I beg my mind to shut down and begin to cry. Rashid holds me tight and whispers,, "You're safe, Kelly."

"Thank you," I whisper. I believe him. My heart hurts because I think he's the one that's not safe. I won't ask him any more questions. We hold each other very tight. I wish the ride to Heathrow would never end. It's raining hard now. My head on his chest, I hear his heart beat, he kisses the top of my head every few minutes. The sound of the rain hitting the roof and windows of the limo wrap around our perfect embrace.

.   .   .

My flight arrives into JFK on time—6:30 p.m. I walk directly to customs—declare nothing. A sense of relief comes over me as I look for the nearest exit. Just as I make my way out I am confronted by two men, badges are produced and I'm in the company of two agents from the CIA. They inform that they have to talk to me and the firmness in the older agent's voice clearly implies options are out. The sense of relief I felt has vanished as I am whisked away to a small office. I can feel my heart pounding as the two humorless men sit me down at a table and begin a barrage of questions. Their demeanor is robotic as they explore my history in great detail.

The lion's share of the questions center on the explosion at the refinery. Then on to identifying photographs of people including five of myself—one with Dan at the Saudi Turf and four from the infamous party. Mr. Al Kahairi, Moktar, Dr. Small, Werner, Steve, Bev and Bob Bruce, Sunil, Dan, Akmed (Tough Guy), Zynab, Carolyn, Jan, and about a dozen photos of Rashid. Most of them are with men I cannot identify. Every picture of him tears at my heart.

Then again back to my life story.

Do I know anything about my birth parents?

Where did I travel to with my parents?

Why an orphanage in Ireland?

How did I get to Yanbu?

Why did I miss my plane in Jeddah?

How did I get out of Yanbu and to Jeddah?

Who made the arrangements?

Did I have a personal relationship with Rashid?

Did I make any phone calls from the Dorchester Hotel—did I receive any?

Then back to the disaster and the infamous party.

Then all of the above again just in a different order.

Three hours later, I'm on a plane headed for Cleveland Hopkins Airport with a few personal items in a Liberty department store bag, an adventure behind me, a head full of questions, an aching heart, and a tender, loving memory of a man with the kind of face you like to rest your eyes on.

Epilogue

September 30, 1987

Dear Angelita,

I hope this letter finds well and happy. Thank you for your kindnesses to me. I really enjoyed your sly humor and bright smile.

I am back home in Ashtabula. My return was facilitated by Rashid - you probably know that. Would you be so kind to write and tell me what happened to a number of people? I have attached a list.

I wish you the very best of everything in life. Keep smiling.

Love,

Kelly

October 21, 1987

Dear Kelly,

So happy to hear from you. I miss you. This is what I know.

Moktar is no longer with the hospital. He is now Coordinator of Logistics for the local Civil Defense Department. He stopped by the hospital recently and asked if anyone has heard from you. Next time I see him, I'll will tell him that I've heard from you, that you have asked about him and I told you of his big new job.

Mr. Al Kahairi remains exactly the same. Carolyn Thomas is still on a month- to- month contract. Jan Hill was deported for indecent dress and intoxication. Sunil is the same and so is Poey. Steve Luney died of cardiac arrest a week ago. Sad to say he had no contact information.

Rumor has it that Dan Gueiterize was deported for making wine in his apartment. Bev Bruce says that when she goes home for Christmas she will not return. But I've heard that before.

I'm really sorry to tell you Fidelis died of AIDS not long after her arrival home in Manila. It was Rashed Zahran who helped get her out of here in a hurry.

About Rashed – I've tried to contact him but he is unreachable. I can't get any information from Kahled. Rashed liked you I know. Maybe you will hear from him. Wouldn't that be nice?

My news- Homer and I plan to be married next month in Manila. The ex- Mrs. Small sent Homer divorce papers instead of the original marriage certificate.

I will keep smiling and you do the same.

Lots of love,

Angelita

CPSIA information can be obtained at www.ICGtesting.com
Printed in the USA
LVOW12s2232190913

353303LV00001B/120/P